Indiscretions

by Donna Hill

Genesis Press, Inc.

315 Third Avenue North
Columbus, Mississippi 39701

Indigo Love Stories

are published by

Genesis Press, Inc.
315 Third Avenue North
Columbus, MS 39701

Indiscretions

ISBN: 1-885478-37-2

Manufactured in the United States of America

Second Edition
Third Printing
Book design by Mary Beth Vickers

Dedication

With all my love...Nichole, Dawne, Matthew and Mahlik. You all are my joy.

Chapter One

As the striking Khendra Phillips moved lithely through Paschal's Lounge, she smiled and waved at the familiar faces—an array of political who's who that habitually frequented the legendary restaurant. Everywhere she went, her self-assurance, classic bronze features, and up-to-the-minute clothes served as a beacon, leading the casual observer to believe she must certainly be a woman of importance. Today was no different. Yet, no one outside of her professional or political circle would ever suspect she was the youngest leading criminal defense attorney in Atlanta, and the only female of her caliber.

Khendra had long ago ceased paying attention to the stares, the admiring glances of men and the envious looks from their dates. In her profession, beauty was not a commodity, and in order to be taken seriously she'd had to be the best—the toughest. It had cost her

dearly in her private life, but her career had soared.

She had come to Paschal's Lounge to meet her friend, Charisse, for lunch. It was said that the whole civil rights struggle had been mapped out in the Cool confines of the restaurant, and it was a known haunt of the young Dr. Martin Luther King, Jr. Regardless of affiliation, however, patrons poured into Paschal's for its exquisite southern cuisine.

Mayor Alan Yancy, who was seated on the far side of the restaurant, noticed Khendra's arrival and raised a hand to gain her attention. Smiling at his ageless face, she threaded her way around the strategically-placed tables to where he sat with three of his aides. They rose as she approached.

"Ms. Phillips," the mayor extended his hand, which she shook, "congratulations on your win today. Assemblyman Daniels couldn't have had better representation."

Nods and low rumbles of approval rounded the table.

"Why thank you," Khendra said, smiling warmly, the acknowledgment from the mayor intensifying her own feelings of success. "I'm just glad it's finally over."

"The prosecution thought they had an airtight case," he added, taking a sip from his glass and giving her a questioning look.

"Nothing is airtight," Khendra stated firmly. "It's simply a matter of making the facts work for or against you."

Alan Yancy pursed his lips and nodded in agreement. "And you have an unparalleled way of doing just that. Won't you join us for lunch?"

"Thank you for asking, but I'm meeting a friend." She turned a slender wrist and checked her watch. "She's late as usual," she added with an amused smile. "Hopefully she'll be here shortly." Khendra's dark brown eyes moved toward the door. "As a matter of fact, I believe she just arrived." She extended her hand to the mayor. He rose to take it. "It was good to see you again, Mayor Yancy."

"I'm sorry you can't join us, but there is one thing I wanted to ask you before you go."

"Yes?" Her silky eyebrows arched in question.

"I understand the firm has taken on the case involving the abortion clinic that was firebombed last month. Will you be handling that one? It's certainly a career maker."

A hush fell over the table. The case had been in the headlines for weeks. Protestors on both sides wanted to be heard. If Khendra said the wrong thing now, it could be politically crippling for the firm. Although she was still fuming from the decision the senior partners had made early that morning, she could not jeopardize

the firm's integrity with her personal opinions. She would deal with them in private. She measured her words before she spoke.

"I'm not at liberty to discuss the case. However, I'm certain the firm will assign the case to whomever it considers most capable."

"I see. Well...I'm sure they will."

"I've really got to be going," she stated apologetically, wanting to get away before any more questions were raised about the case, and she lost the control she had been struggling to maintain all morning.

"Of course, and continued success to you, Ms. Phillips. I look forward to hearing extraordinary things about you."

"Thank you."

With that, she successfully made her escape and headed toward her table. All the while, that last question burned through her brain. Why did they have to ask about the clinic? She had been trying since that morning—when the name Sean Michaels had been tossed at her like a gauntlet—to keep that case out of her thoughts. She was still reeling from the early morning conference with the senior partners. It had taken all of her concentration to keep focused on her closing argument, as visions of the heated meeting kept cropping up whenever she let her guard down. She still could not accept the firm's decision to turn the case over to a new-

4

comer. The injustice of what had been done to her ignited anew, snuffing her recent victory.

She took her seat at the table, just as Charisse,
totally nonplussed by her late arrival, was being seated.

"Whew, this heat is unbelievable," Charisse
breathed in her throaty, southern twang. She slipped her
dark sunglasses off and immediately lit a cigarette, a
habit which Khendra deplored but had grown weary of
discussing with Charisse. Khendra sat back and shook
her head in reproach, which Charisse pointedly ignored.

Through clouds of smoke, Charisse, in her
straightforward manner, got right to the point. "I know
you won the case. It's all over the radio and television.
So why do you look like your mother just died?"

"Thanks. You always were the messenger of
good cheer," Khendra said dryly.

"Just being honest, hon. So what's up?"
Charisse asked, as the waitress appeared.

Charisse ordered a platter of buffalo wings, the
house salad and a glass of lemonade. Khendra ordered
a coke. Then she began to recant the events of the
morning.

"...how dare they?" Khendra fumed. "I should
have gotten that case!" She leaned forward on the table,
her agitation barely held in check as she spoke in a
pained voice. "Do you know what it feels like to have
one of the biggest criminal cases come your way and

then have your bosses tell you that they're hiring an attorney from New York, and he's going to handle the case?"

Charisse took a long swallow of her ice-cold lemonade and shook her dark head. "Girl, you've been going through this for the last three years. You just nevah learn, do you? You gotta learn how to play the game, girl," Charisse said in a conspiratorial whisper, while blowing a cloud of smoke in the air. "How many times have I told you that? You cain't keep marching around with your screw the status quo attitude and expect the big boys to go along with it."

Khendra blew out an exasperated breath. "Don't you understand Charisse?" she cut in before Charisse could get on a roll. "Law is my life, my love. I've wanted to be an attorney for as long as I can remember. Just because I don't follow protocol doesn't mean I should be passed over like an old shoe. And for a man at that!"

Charisse let out a short laugh. "That's part of your problem, hon. Maybe if law wasn't your life and your love you wouldn't be so obsessed with it, and get so bent out of shape when things like this happen." She took another sip of lemonade and nodded her head to the waitress as she placed the platter of food on the table.

She took a forkful of the mouth-watering salad

and dipped a wing in the tangy, white sauce. "There's more to life than work," she said between bites. "Mmm, you really should try this. It's delicious." She briefly lifted her eyes from her plate and raised her eyebrows in question, while Khendra sat absently twirling the straw in her coke.

Khendra shook her head. "I really wish you wouldn't talk to me with a mouth full of food. This is important, Charisse."

"All right, all right." Charisse put her fork down on the plate, placed her hands on her chin, and leaned on her elbows, feigning rapt attention. "This better?"

Khendra tossed her head back in laughter, and tapped Charisse on the head with her napkin. "You're crazy. I don't know how I put up with you. But seriously, you know that relationships have never been easy for me," Khendra said in a soft voice. "Being a junior in college at sixteen had its good points and its drawbacks. When girls my age were out learning the fine points of socializing, my head was stuck in a book. I never felt comfortable with the boys my age. We had nothing in common. The guys in my classes felt that even though I was as smart as they were—"

"Smarter," Charisse cut in.

Khendra smiled. "—I wasn't old enough for them. And now, well—" Her voice trailed off and she looked away.

"But everybody needs somebody to come home to."

"I had someone. Remember?" she said, the pain still evident in her voice.

Charisse reached over and patted her hand. "I know," she said softly. "I'm sorry for being such an insensitive so-and-so. I shouldn't have said that."

Khendra turned to face her lifelong friend. "I know you didn't mean any harm."

"It's just that," Charisse began, "I'm sure Tony wouldn't have wanted you to still be in mourning, Khen. It's been over a year."

"You're probably right." Her eyes trailed off to search the horizon. "You usually are, as much as I hate to admit it," she sniffed, dabbing at her eyes with the napkin. She gave Charisse a lopsided grin. "But I have my work, and that's what's important now," she replied, sounding stronger than she actually felt. "This case could have solidified my career."

"So what are you going to do?"

"I don't know." She lowered her head and expelled a deep sigh. "I've toyed with the idea of leaving and going elsewhere. I even told them as much this morning."

"You did?" Charisse was shocked. McMahon, Counts and Perry was the leading law firm in the State of Georgia. This job meant everything to Khendra.

True, she suffered occasional kicks in the backside, but for Khendra to even consider leaving must mean she had really had enough. Now Charisse was really worried.

She had known Khendra since they were five years old, growing up in the Atlanta housing projects. Even then, Khendra wanted to be an attorney, and assumed the role of peacemaker between the children on the street when they were involved in fights. She had always been "different" everyone said. It wasn't until she started school that they realized what the difference was. Khendra was brilliant. While everyone else struggled through school, Khendra skipped grades. Then, attending the prestigious all-girls' Spelman College didn't help her social prowess either. By the time she was twenty, she had graduated from law school in the top five percent of her class. And in the following year she had passed the bar exam in both Georgia and New York.

To many men, Khendra was intimidating and a threat to their manhood. Not only was she beautiful—which she never seemed to realize—she was smart as well. A devastating combination. Yet, there were still those diehard few who would give their right and left arms just for some acknowledgment from her. But as Khendra had often said, she had never learned how to deal with men other than on a business level. The one time she tried, she had been devastated by the outcome and still blamed herself. She had so much to offer, but it was going to take a special man to help her realize that. Trying to help her find that man was a quest Charisse avidly pursued.

"What was the response of the mighty ones when you told them you were considering leaving?"

Khendra sighed deeply and stirred her coke. "Mr. McMahon said, 'Well, Ms. Phillips,'" Khendra mocked in a low grumble, "'we will certainly miss you, but you have to do what you think is best.'"

"Damn!" Charisse swore under her breath. "It would serve them right if you did leave. You can do better someplace else. Why don't you try some of the other law firms? You've had plenty of offers. What about that guy, Cliff something-or-other, in New York, who just started a firm? I'd miss you like hell, but at least I'd have a vacation spot. Go someplace where you'll be appreciated. You've put up with enough of this crap."

"I have to stay. I only said that to get their reactions."

"Yeah, and look what you got," she added, taking a bite of chicken.

"I know, but I have something to prove, Charisse. Not just to myself, but to my family and to them. My folks never believed that I could make it in a predominantly white male profession." Her smooth brow furrowed in contemplation. "And I know that this whole stunt is the firm's way of keeping me in my place. They've never made it a secret that they haven't been pleased with my handling of the press on my previous cases. If and when I do decide to leave," she said, her voice picking up strength and determination as she spoke, "it'll be on my terms," she shook her auburn head vehemently, "not on theirs."

Charisse smiled, satisfied that Khendra would come out on top of this dilemma as she had all of the others. When the tide turned against Khendra, she was at her best. Charisse just wished she was as persevering in her love life as she was in her career. She was dynamite in the courtroom, but her success with men could use a good shot in the arm.

"Now that's the girl I know," Charisse said, smiling brightly. "But listen, hon," she checked her watch and took a forkful of food, "I've really got to get back to the boutique. If I don't, those salesgirls will run me in the poorhouse, selling things that ain't on sale!" She slapped her hand down on the table and let out a throaty laugh. "So I'll see you soon. Hear? Give me a call. I've got this great guy that you'd just love."

Khendra twisted her lips and shook her head in defeat. Charisse's life revolved around men and romance. It was a rare occasion when Charisse wasn't in love with love. Most people couldn't understand how they had remained friends for so many years. They were as different as night and day. That was probably the attraction. Charisse provided the excitement, while Khendra was the level-headed one. But maybe a date would do her good. It had been a long while. At least it would be a diversion from her usual routine.

"O.k. I'll call you,'" she conceded. We'll plan something."

"Soon," Charisse said firmly as she slid out of her seat, smoothing her white cotton skirt over her full hips. She slipped her dark shades over her broad nose, and leaned over to give Khendra a peck on the cheek. My treat," she said, placing a twenty dollar bill on the table. "And don't forget, I'll be waiting to hear from you," she called over her shoulder as she made her exit.

Khendra waved goodbye and blew a kiss. When she had finished her Coke, she paid the check and headed back to her office.

⊸⧽⧼⊷

Khendra stood momentarily in front of her office building, looking up at the unimaginative blocks of concrete and glass. Maybe that was why she was always so avant-garde in her mode of dress, she mused, looking down at her canary yellow, linen skirt and brown paisley blazer. Perhaps it was her way of breathing life, vitality and a splash of color into the drab, gray world of the legal profession. But her flamboyant nature and outspoken manner had cost her, she realized. Yet, she still refused to totally bend to the will of her superiors, no matter what they did to her.

Although her anger had subsided somewhat after talking with Charisse, it began to once again boil to the surface as she made the slow rise on the elevator. At some point, she knew she would have to confront the false faces of the other attorneys, with all of them knowing full well how she had been slighted. A dull throb pumped methodically in her right temple when she envisioned the questions, the looks.

This was the first time she could recall doubting herself. Self-doubt regarding her profession was an emotion with which she was totally unfamiliar. On the other hand, she knew from day one that as soon as she stepped through the hallowed halls of McMahon, Counts and Perry, she was going to have to work harder than anyone in the firm. Although her credentials spoke for themselves, she was the first black female associate ever hired in the firm's 104-year history. They took a chance with her and she knew it. But her nonconformist nature would not allow her to be molded into their conventional approach to criminal defense, which was her specialty. This, compounded with her opinionated persona, kept her constantly in hot water with the

Donna Hill

senior partners. Inwardly she cringed when the words she had lashed out at them whipped through her brain— spineless, visionless— The recollection and the inevitable aftermath made her throbbing head spin.

❧

Walking briskly through the hushed corridors, her mind totally entrenched in her latest dilemma, she made the sharp right turn toward her office and walked smack into what she swore had to be a recently-erected wall. Her portfolio flew out of her hand and its contents spilled out on the carpeted floor.

"I'm so sorry...I wasn't...I didn't—" she blurted out in an embarrassed jumble, realizing that it was a person and not a thing she had collided with. She blindly stooped down to retrieve the scattered articles. As she gathered the materials in a pile, a warm, masculine hand covered hers, and a voice with the soul-stirring resonance of a gospel singer stroked her rattled nerves.

"Let me. It was partly my fault, anyway."

Khendra's eyes slowly rose and rested upon the most smoldering black eyes she had ever seen. They appeared to dance with mischief, and something more—something dangerously inviting.

"Are you all right?" he asked, the beginnings of a dimpled smile easing across his smooth face. When a

14

full smile lit up his face, Khendra felt herself dissolve like melted butter, as perfect milky-white teeth sparkled against his deep, dark chocolate complexion.

"Yes...I'm fine.   Thank you," she answered slowly. *Who was that person who just sounded like Minnie Mouse?*

He extended a hand to her, helping her to rise from her crouched position.   She gingerly placed her hand in his and immediately felt the tingle of electricity creep through her body. His eyes and his smile held her entranced as she rose to meet his piercing gaze.

He stood a full head taller than she in her two-inch heels, which would place him at about six feet three inches, she quickly surmised.   His appearance bore the impression of a sleek panther—lethally quick and sensual.   He wore his dark hair cut very close, allowing the natural waves to show through. His broad shoulders filled the obviously-expensive suit exquisitely, leading her to feel he would look good not only in a board room, but on a football field as well. Just his look and the way his half-smile played around his full lips made her feel totally vulnerable and completely feminine, feelings that were gently disturbing. The only way she knew how to handle the situation was in a business-like manner, though her insides yearned for another approach.

"Are you looking for someone? Perhaps I can

point you in the right direction," she said, a part of her hoping they were heading the same way.

"Actually," he began somewhat sheepishly, "I'm heading toward my office."

Her eyebrows lifted in surprise. "Really? I guess this is my day for getting caught off guard."

"Excuse me?" He gave her a curious look.

"Nothing. Just thinking out loud. So...where is your office?"

"Right down the hall, I think." He pulled a card from the breast pocket of his midnight blue suit. "According to the receptionist, my office is opposite a Khendra Phillips'. Do you know her?"

Khendra's stomach fluttered. "Very well, actually. I'm Khendra Phillips." She gave him a tentative smile. "And you are—?"

He returned her smile. "So you're the formidable Ms. Phillips." He was pleased by the bright colors she wore, which were totally in contrast to the somber hues that pervaded the legal industry. His eyes quickly slid over her curvaceous figure, as he concentrated hard to keep his mind focused on the conversation at hand.

"I've heard great stories about your legal wizardry." His satiny voice caressed her statuesque form as he spoke. "The newspaper photos do you no justice."

As his dark eyes once again roamed over her body, Khendra had the dizzying sensation of being stripped bare under his heated gaze. A slow throb pumped steadily inside her, as though warning her of the unseen danger that lingered behind those volcanic orbs. Then that heart-stopping voice brought her back to reality.

"It's nice to finally meet you. I'm Sean Michaels." Khendra's smile slowly dissolved.

"Problem?" His brows creased at her sudden change in expression.

So this was Sean Michaels! The hot-shot attorney from New York who had stolen a golden opportunity from her. Her anger rushed to the surface in waves.

"I guess I don't feel too formidable today," she answered curtly.

His thick eyebrows rose in surprise. "Tough case?"

"No. Tough politics." She gave him a cutting smile. "I've really got to be going, Mr. Michaels." She started to move away.

"Maybe you'd like to talk about it," he called out to her retreating back.

She stopped and turned toward him, confusion and surprise outlining her eyes.

"That is, if you want to. I have a very sympathetic ear." He shifted the stack of briefs under his arm and gave her the most unsettling look as he waited for her response.

Donna Hill

"I don't know if that—"

"How about this? Why don't I take you to dinner when we sign off?" He shrugged his left shoulder
and tilted his head to the side, looking at her through
dark lashes. "We can talk about anything you like. No
shop talk." When she didn't respond, he added, "I could
really do with some beautiful company. It gets pretty
lonely when you're new in town."

She almost let herself forget who he was, as she
felt herself being slowly swallowed up in the hypnotic
cadence of his voice, the magic of his smile. Then she
quickly regained her senses. *He's good, real good. He
almost had me fooled for a minute.*

"I doubt it very seriously, Mr. Michaels. I'm
sure I'm not the kind of company you're looking for."

"Why? Are you married?"

"No." She suddenly felt flustered by the pos-
sessive way he looked at her—very casual, but unyield-
ing. "Anyway, I don't think my personal life is any of
your business," she snapped, feeling as if she had to
defend herself.

He tilted his chin up and observed her from an
angle, trying hard to keep a smile from forming. "I see.
Well, I'll be here until six," he said smoothly, not in the
least put off by her cool demeanor.

"You seem very sure of yourself, Mr. Michaels."

"That's what makes me so good at what I do."

His eyes burned into hers. "And you can call me Sean."

He's an arrogant—but she wouldn't let the words form in her head. "I'll think about both." Khendra tucked her portfolio securely under her arm. "And by the way, you're headed in the wrong direction," she added, feeling the infantile need to knock him off his pedestal. She proceeded down the corridor, never once looking back at the figure that continued to stare at her.

Sean chuckled inwardly, while carelessly leaning against the wall, watching her graceful movements. He was fascinated by the luxurious auburn hair that hung loosely on her proud shoulders. The seductive swaying of her slightly rounded hips beneath her blazer assured him that fire lay beneath her polished surface. Her skin tone reminded him of the finest brandy when held up to the light.

Yes, he had to get to know this very interesting woman and find out if she was everything he had heard she was, and what he had done to cause the glint of challenge that lit those earthy brown eyes. He was sure that beneath her cool exterior, there was much, much more. He was determined to unleash it. After all, they were neighbors, and maybe when they got to know each other he would find the something he so desperately needed in his life. As long as it didn't interfere with his plans.

Chapter Two

Khendra entered her office and gently closed the door behind her. She was fully aware that Mr. Sean Michaels' eyes were recording her every movement and she was determined to show him that he hadn't affected her in the least—a monumental feat, considering her heart was hammering in her chest like an automated set of African drums.

She leaned against the closed door, briefly shut her eyes, and took a calming breath. So he thought he could just stroll in, steal her thunder and then charm her out of her shoes. Well, Mr. Sean Michaels had another think coming! She was his equal on every level and she'd prove it. Maybe she would take him up on his offer of dinner, just to show him a thing or two.

She marched toward her desk, then halted midway. *Stop deluding yourself,* she thought, slowly releasing her clenched jaw. A soft smile of realization formed around her lips. *You know good and well Sean Michaels is one of the most devastatingly handsome men you've set your eyes on in a long time. And his getting the case has nothing to do with how fast your heart is racing. Let's face it, it wasn't his fault the firm chose him to handle that particular case. How could he know the inner workings of MC&P?*

She had judged him unfairly, she admitted, without giving him a chance. But why in heaven's name did the very man who could steal her glorious reign have to be the same man who had just made her feel all the sensations she thought she had buried with all the other memories?

She knew she would have to be careful. If his stunning good looks and smooth conversation were any indication of his personality, he'd probably just as soon slide into her bed as stab her in the back to get ahead. She had met his type before and remembered all too well.

There you go again, she warned herself. She took a deep breath and mentally repeated the litany Charisse had implanted in her brain..."Every man is not out to get something. Just be the jury and not the judge!"

She rounded her desk and slipped down into her worn leather chair, deciding she would at least give him the benefit of the doubt, unless he proved he didn't deserve her trust. She was going to be practical, she concluded. But when she visualized how he had looked at her, thrilling sparks of current raced through her veins, tossing all rationale out the window.

It had been a long time since she had felt such a powerful attraction to a man, and the awareness shook her to her very core. Yet, there was still that part of her that felt she was betraying Tony's memory. That was the most difficult emotion to shake.

Her conflicting thoughts were momentarily interrupted by the beep of her intercom. She reluctantly pulled herself back to the present and pressed the flashing light.

"Yes, Leslie?"

"Ms. Phillips, District Attorney Damato is here to see you."

"Send him in momentarily, Leslie. And bring the file in with you. Oh, and Les, please bring your pad also. I want you to sit in on this meeting and take notes."

"Certainly."

Thoughts of Sean Michaels would have to wait.

Sean stepped into his new office, and immediately felt he had finally arrived. The finely crafted mahogany desk was only the beginning. A lush oriental carpet covered most of the highly-polished parquet floor. A sleek, burgundy leather sofa graced one wall of the tastefully-decorated room.

He was most impressed with the view. One twirl of the wand that opened the blinds, and the entire city spanned before his eyes. Atlanta was a beautiful and powerful metropolis and he was determined to make his mark. This job was going to be the turning point in his life. A time to start over and put the past behind him for good.

He moved self-assuredly through the room, acquainting himself with his space. Stopping, he placed the briefs on his desk, and ran his hand possessively across the polished surface. Slowly, he lowered himself down into the burgundy, antique leather chair, his dark eyes roaming the room in wonder.

Things had to be different this time. No more taking a back seat to anyone. He'd had enough of that in New York. He was starting here with an excellent track record and he didn't owe anyone any favors. He intended to keep it that way. All the bad memories were behind him. A slight shudder of remembrance raced up his broad back. He could still see the headlines, hear the questions.

But this was his new beginning, he thought, taking a cleansing breath. He intended to take every opportunity that came his way and capitalize on it.

He spun slowly in his chair. Then like a child let loose in a toy store, he seemed to lose control and spun round and round in total euphoria. A smile of complete satisfaction beamed across his face. When he and the chair came to a stop, he looked up to see Khendra standing in the open doorway, a half-smile forming on her full, rich lips.

"We've all been through it, you know." She stepped partially into the room and looked boldly around. "When I first came here I thought I had died and gone to attorney's heaven." She smiled openly now and Sean joined her with a smile of his own.

He stood up and moved from behind his desk, sticking his hands in his pockets as he approached. "So, Ms. Phillips, we do have something in common."

Khendra immediately felt the change in the atmosphere. The heat of uncertainty coursed through her veins. She felt suddenly out of her league with him, and she instantly put up her protective shield. "I didn't say that," she uttered defensively. "I just meant that—"

"What are you afraid of? It couldn't possibly be me." He moved closer, his eyes never leaving hers.

"I'm not afraid of anything, Mr. Michaels." She defiantly jutted out her strong chin. "I was only making an observation. You're very presumptuous." She turned on her heel to leave.

"So are we on for dinner or not?"

She threw him a threatening look and slammed out of the door, her heart thudding with every movement.

Sean shook his head in amusement. He returned to his desk and leaned back in his chair. You're a pretty tough lady, Ms. Phillips, but you ain't seen nothin' yet.

Khendra returned to her office, her breathing coming in rapid bursts. She balled her hands into small fists and swung them back toward the closed door, wishing she could knock that self-satisfied smile off of his face. But what good would that do? she thought, her sanity returning. He would probably just have a smooth response and make her feel like a complete fool, like he had done from the moment she set eyes on him. Who did he think he was anyway, with his playboy looks and Kool-Aid smile?

She let out an exasperated breath and plopped down into her chair. Well, she would just stay clear of him. But what was it about him that made her lose control? Was it those eyes that crinkled at the corners when he smiled? she mused. Was it the way those dimples gave him the look of an innocent little boy? Or was it simply the way he made her feel—so vulnerable and soft inside?

What was happening to her? She had never let a man affect her this way before. At least not since Tony, she thought, the old knot of pain boiling up in her stomach. And she wouldn't let it happen again. She would definitely have to get a grip on her feelings, especially if they had to work together. She could not allow him to continually throw her off balance. It was totally unprofessional, she decided with finality.

Her thoughts were interrupted by the buzzing of her intercom. She snapped out of her musings and pressed the flashing red light.

"Yes, Leslie?"

"Ms. Phillips, Mr. Counts is here to see you," she said, the awe obvious in her voice.

Khendra was momentarily stunned into silence. *Alex Counts?* It was common knowledge that he was the power behind McMahon, Counts & Perry. He never so much as smiled at the associates, and had never, as long as she could recall, ever been down on "associates' row," as her floor had been dubbed. What in the world could he want with her?

Then it hit her. He was probably here to personally escort her out of the building. She had said some pretty nasty things at the meeting that morning. Oh, Lordy, she was going to be totally humiliated. Well, if that was the way it was to be, she would walk out with

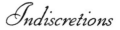

her head held high.

"Send him right in, Leslie," she answered firmly.

Quickly she straightened her desk, took a deep breath, and pretended she was going over a case transcript as Alex Counts entered the room.

Alex Counts' imposing presence seemed to absorb the energy from the tiny office and radiate it back through his electric blue eyes. He had thick steel-gray hair and his solid build reflected a man of enormous power and control. But Khendra was not intimidated. She barely looked up as he made his entrance.

Alex closed the door softly behind him, but did not step fully into the room. He very subtly took in the artsy interior of the office, noting the African sculptures that graced the credenza and the tasteful framed artwork hanging on the walls. Then a slow, uncharacteristic smile crept onto his otherwise stony features.

"Very interesting office, Ms. Phillips." He unbuttoned the jacket of his gray suit and openly viewed his surroundings. "It is most certainly a reflection of you."

"I don't know if that's a compliment or an insult at this point, Mr. Counts."

This time he gave in to a deep laugh, making Khendra's eyebrows rise in surprise.

"Believe me, it was meant as a compliment.

May I sit down?"

"Please do," she answered, indicating the long sofa with a nod of her head. *What is going on here?*

Alex Counts took a seat and stretched an arm across its back. "Ms. Phillips, I'd like to get straight to the point. A lot of things were said this morning. Some of them made sense, others didn't. What you said in that conference room hit home, as much as we hate to admit it. I don't think we even realized our true motivations, but you made us see them. Those are the qualities that make you such a brilliant attorney. We'd be bigger asses than you think we are, if we let you leave."

Khendra shifted in her chair with as much nonchalance as she could summon. "What are you saying exactly, Mr. Counts?" she asked slowly.

"I'm saying... we're saying that we want you to stay on with the firm. And," he stood up and walked toward her desk, "I'd be more than willing to back you for a partnership at the end of our next quarter. Of course, you realize that with my endorsement it would virtually be guaranteed."

Khendra was stunned. Her ploy had worked better than she could have possibly anticipated. Now, not only would she not have to eat her words, but Mr. Counts was offering his support for a partnership. As her spirits soared, her mind raced in every direction. She felt like a tight coil ready to spring. But she kept her excitement in check. There had to be a catch.

"Why the end of the next quarter? Why not now?" she asked as calmly as she could.

"We'll be doing a lot of revamping within the next three months. As you know, Mr. McMahon will be retiring shortly. That leaves a senior partner slot open, which we intend to fill with one of the junior partners. That leaves a junior partner position open."

Khendra pursed her lips and slowly rose from her seat. She had to play this right or she would blow it. *Slow down, girl, and don't let your mouth run faster than your brain.* "How much time do I get to think about this, Mr. Counts?"

For a brief second, he looked shocked, which pleased Khendra tremendously. She mustn't let him think she was too eager.

"Think about it? I thought you would be more than happy to get a solid shot at a partnership."

"Under the circumstances, I'd like some time to think it over. It's hard for me to digest, especially after our earlier meeting. You must admit, this is a big turnaround." Her face remained unreadable.

"I see," he said, as though reconsidering his approach. This wouldn't be as easy as he thought. "I can assure you that my offer is airtight. And your salary, of course, would be doubled."

Khendra moved slowly from behind her desk. A

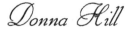

partnership, she thought. This was what she had dreamed of, what she had worked so hard to obtain. But she had just been burned by the firm that morning. She had to proceed with caution. She looked Alex squarely in the eyes, her voice firm, her heart quaking.

"I'll get back to you by the end of the week. Is that satisfactory?" She knew she was pushing her luck, but she was going to play it out. If they wanted her badly enough, they would wait for her decision.

"Ms. Phillips," Alex gave her a conceding smile, "you're a tough negotiator. I look forward to hearing from you by the end of the week."

"Thank you, Mr. Counts. For the offer," she added, giving him her most professional smile. She extended a well-manicured hand, relief flowing through her.

Instead of shaking her hand, Alex brought it to his lips and placed a warm kiss across her knuckles. Then, ever so slowly, he released her hand from his grasp. Khendra remained impassive, her disbelief rendering her immobile.

"You intrigue me, Khendra." It was the first time he had said her given name, and he instantly liked the sound of it rolling off his lips. "I'd like the opportunity to get to know you better. Perhaps over dinner some evening?"

His question sounded more like a statement to

her startled ears. "Perhaps, Mr. Counts. However, I couldn't begin to think about that right now. I'm sure you can understand that." She drew herself up to her full five-feet, eight-inch height, jutting her chin forward in a firm gesture.

"Of course," he said, his interest mounting in this prepossessing young woman. "You have a lot of potential. You're one of the best criminal attorneys I've seen in a long time. And believe me, I've seen them come and go." He gave her an intimate look. "I could, personally, see to it that your career goes a long way...Khendra." With that he turned and strode out of the office.

This was getting more curious by the minute. Khendra sat back down, trying to absorb the implications of the conversation. She kept coming up with the same answers. But she had to be wrong. Alex Counts was a married man. Maybe she misread him. Yes, that had to be it.

However, if she decided to see this thing through, it would have to be her way, and she would never allow herself to be at the mercy of Alex Counts. She couldn't...wouldn't compromise her values, not even for the job of her dreams. She had a lot of thinking to do, and four days to do it in. Then that catchall phrase came back to her, "...it's airtight." Nothing is airtight, she reminded herself once again. Nothing at all.

Chapter Three

Fighting off waves of exhaustion, Khendra waded through the stacks of notes and transcripts that decorated her well-worn desk, pushing the events of the day to the back of her mind. She worked steadily for hours, poring over the pages in front of her. Periodically she made comments into her tape recorder and hastily scribbled others on her yellow pad. She continued to work until the shadow of evening fell over her shoulders. Pulling herself up from her huddled position, she rolled her neck to relieve the stiffness. She removed her square, red-rimmed glasses and stretched her slender arms high above her head.

As if awakening from a trance, she realized it had grown unusually dark and the normally-busy hallways were all but silent. She could just make out the far-off sounds of the methodic tapping of a printer and the tinkling bell of the elevator as it touched down on her floor.

Shaking her head to clear the cobwebs, she checked her watch and realized it was only six-fifteen. Where was everyone? Six o'clock was almost lunchtime for many of the attorneys who worked at MC&P. Then, in a flash of recollection, it came back to her. Leslie had said hours ago that everyone was leaving early due to the storm warnings that had been issued on the news service. She vaguely remembered nodding her response and waving Leslie away with a toss of her hand. She had been so engrossed in her work, she hadn't really given the warning any attention.

Now, her large brown eyes swept toward the window. The sunless sky was nearly black. Heavy, ominous clouds hovered above like hungry vultures, waiting to release a barrage on the hapless victims beneath. Her eyes trailed to the street below, watching in fascination as the glare of car lights bit across the gray concrete, silhouetting the anxious commuters as they hurried home to safety.

Home, Khendra thought with a reluctant sigh, turning away from the window. Home...just another place to be alone. At least here in the office and in the courtroom there were the noises, the phones, the cases. At home, there were only memories and endless hours until tomorrow.

She slept better now, she thought absently, slipping her notes into her briefcase. At least the ache was dull, the edge gone. She didn't wake up at night with that empty sensation. And she had long ago stopped asking herself why? It was better this way, she had concluded. No attachments, no loss, no pain. Her work was enough.

She reached for her jacket hanging on the brass coat rack, just as a blast of thunder roared through the heavens. It seemed like everything vibrated at once, including her heart. It was on a night very much like this one that—*No!* She wouldn't think about it. Not again. As she shook her head to rid her memory of those haunting images, a bolt of lightning illuminated the sky. Any moment now the heavens would open, Khendra thought, grabbing her briefcase and jacket in one swoop.

She walked to the door, opened it, and turned to look over her office. Satisfied that she hadn't forgotten anything, she locked the door and headed for the elevator. She pressed the button marked "G" and the elevator quietly descended to the garage level beneath the building. On a night like tonight, a parking space in the building was one luxury she could truly appreciate.

The garage was nearly empty. Only a few cars dotted the underground cavern. The only sound was the click of her heels reverberating throughout the tunnel—bouncing off the pillars and back again as if to keep her

company.

Just as she reached her black Volvo and started to insert the key into the door lock, she heard the roar of an engine and was instantly caught in the glare of oncoming lights. The car was coming straight toward her at full speed. She couldn't move. For a hysterical moment, she reacted like a fawn on a highway, paralyzed by the headlights. She automatically shut her eyes, fearing the worst. Then, just as abruptly as it had appeared, the car came to a screeching halt alongside her car. Relieved, she opened her eyes and set them on none other than Sean Michaels. How many times in one day would she wish that she could smack him?

He stepped out of the driver's side of his silver BMW and carelessly leaned across the hood. His ebony eyes remained fixed on the face he hadn't been able to get out of his head all day.

"I was waiting for you," he said easily.

Her heart skipped a beat. "What for?" She wanted to feel angry, but instead was suddenly flattered.

He glided around the front of his car and stood beside her. The scent of his cologne raced through her senses, leaving her feeling weak and breathless. She instinctively took a step backwards and averted her eyes. Fighting to control the tremor in her hand, she attempted to insert the key once again. She had to get away. But in one leisurely motion he plucked the key from her nerveless fingers and slid it into the tiny lock. He was so close to her now, she could swear she heard his heart hammering against his chest. Or was it her heart?

"Weren't you going to wait for my answer?" He pulled the door open and handed her the key.

She could feel the heat of his breath brush across her cheek. A flutter pumped through her insides. "Not really." She clasped the key in her hand and stooped to get into her car. "It was a rhetorical question." She refused to look at him.

He placed a hand on her shoulder, stalling her. "I'll answer you anyway." His voice was so deep, it seemed to reach down to her toes and thread its way up through her every muscle, making them feel like hot, melting wax. "I wanted to see you."

Those simple words rocketed through her, rendering her speechless. She had to look at him now, to see if his words were sincere. She took that chance, and this time she knew that the sound she heard was the echo of her own heart dancing inside her chest.

"Why would you want to see me?" Her voice sounded childlike, her eyes were wide with uncertainty.

"I mean, I was rather rude earlier," she added half-apologetically.

"Really? I hadn't noticed." A teasing smile spread across his lips and lit candles in his eyes.

"Maybe we got off on the wrong foot. I'd like to make up for that. If you'll let me."

She lowered her eyes, then looked up at him. A slow smile graced her face. Then, she quickly caught herself. "It's getting late. I really have to get home."

"Why?" The question was so blunt and unexpected, it stunned her. For several seconds, she let it hang noiselessly in the air.

"It's...it's just that...I—"

"Is being home alone on a hot, stormy night better than enjoying some good food, some soft music and a few laughs with a co-worker and potential friend?" His eyes roamed over her face as he spoke, riveting her with their intensity. "I wasn't lying when I said I could use some beautiful company."

Khendra resented his presumptuousness. How dare he assume that she would be home alone. Her mind raced through the assortment of excuses she had stock-piled for occasions such as this. But for some reason she didn't want to use any of them, and the realization frightened her.

"Well...I guess—"

"Great! You know your way around better than I do, so you drive." Before she could utter a protest, he had slipped around to the passenger side of the car and seated himself.

For a moment she simply stood there, motionless. Her mouth opened, then shut when she could find no words to fit her discomfiture. She shook her head, and in spite of herself, she burst out laughing. As she slipped behind the wheel of her car, she thought, He's a real character.

High winds whipped through the trees, turning over trash cans and rattling windows. Pouring rain pummeled the ground, hitting the pavement so hard the drops seemed to dance before they settled. Water ran in rapid streams down the steamy streets. However, Khendra and Sean were totally unaffected. The intimate atmosphere of the restaurant provided the perfect hide-away from the wrath of mother nature. The soft glow of the tabletop candles gave the spacious dining room a cozy atmosphere. Tiny tables, dotted with pink linen tablecloths, were equally dispersed throughout the room, allowing all of the diners a semblance of privacy. A small dance floor was the focal point. Soft music, being played by a small jazz combo, emanated from a corner of the room.

Khendra sat across the table from Sean, feeling pleasantly surprised. She was totally at ease with him. His easy manner and wry wit kept her continually amused. He had a natural way of making her smile. He also had a very serious side, she discovered, when he revealed bits of information about his childhood.

"Where did you grow up, Sean?" Khendra had asked between tiny bites of the succulent steak, and sips of Coke.

"Most of my life I lived in New York, in Harlem, actually."

"Really? Where?"

"Right on 135th Street and Lenox Avenue."

"You were certainly in the heart of it."

"You can say that again. Most of the guys I grew up with didn't make it out of there. I guess I was lucky."

"What happened to your friends?"

Sean took a bite of his braised chicken before he spoke. "Most of them were either killed, or jailed, or strung out by the time I was in my teens." His eyes held a faraway look as he spoke. "I guess that's when I first became interested in law. There seemed, to me, no way to beat the system, so I felt the only way I could do any good was to become a part of it. And maybe, somehow, find a way to change it. I saw so many young brothers and sisters become victims. When I first started out, I believed the way to fight all of the injustices was as a legal aid, helping those who couldn't afford to get outside legal help."

"Well, you're along way from that ideation,"

Khendra remarked, somewhat perplexed by his present course in law.

Sean smiled. "It was either that or starve. I guess I became somewhat jaded as well. When you see so much destruction going on around you every day, you tend to lose your perspective. But eventually, I intend to open my own law firm, specifically for the poor. That's one of the main reasons I came here."

"I don't understand."

"Money. Plain and simple. This position can provide me with the financial security and nobility I'll need to get off on my own."

"What are the other reasons?" Khendra asked, her interest peaked.

It was too soon to open himself up to her completely, Sean thought. He didn't want to scare her away. How she felt about him became suddenly important. "I'd rather not talk about it right now, if you don't mind," he said softly. "Maybe some other time."

"All right," she said, secretly pleased. At least he had said "some other time," and the thought of another evening with Sean made her feel warm and excited inside.

They talked of inconsequential things then— music, their favorite movies, places they had been and things they had seen—the friction of their earlier meeting temporarily forgotten. The flickering flame from the warm candles seemed to accent the mood, and compliment the rise of complex feelings they were both experiencing.

As the band started a rendition of Grover Washington, Jr.'s *Mr. Magic*, Sean reached for her hand. "That's my man," he said, tapping his foot to the pulsing beat. And before Khendra knew what was happening, he had pulled her out of her seat and swept her onto the dance floor.

He held her close, gliding her effortlessly across the smooth wooden floor with the grace of a polished dancer, as he hummed in perfect tune to the music. Khendra felt his every muscle as they pressed against her. Inch by inch, she felt her insides ignite with sensations she didn't know still existed within her. She suddenly felt safe and secure in his arms. His heady scent and the comforting warmth of him held her enthralled. She forgot to be wary and simply let herself be swept away in his embrace.

When the song ended, he held onto her for a second too long, looking into her eyes as if seeing her for the first time. Her heart stood still—waiting. Then he looked away and the spell was broken. He took her hand in his and escorted her back to their table.

He was a maze of conflicts, Khendra realized as she took her seat and forced her legs to stop trembling. One moment he seemed like the international gigolo, the next, one of the most considerate and gentle men she had ever met. She was totally confused. She so wanted to find something to hold against him, to help her ward off the throbbing impulses he created within her. But she no longer could, and the split second of irrefutability quickened her pulse. Oh Lordy, she didn't want to be a victim again. Not again.

"So tell me about you," Sean said, breaking into her thoughts. "You've heard my boring life story." He gave her an encouraging smile.

"There's not much to tell, really." She averted her eyes, keeping them focused on the glass in her hands.

"I'm sure you've had an interesting life. What about school, family, old boyfriends?" He took a sip of mineral water and waited.

"Well...I was a recluse in school. I guess these days, I would be considered a nerd." She laughed nervously.

"I can't imagine you being anything but extraordinary," he said softly, the look in his eyes making her stomach do flips.

She shrugged her shoulders and gave a half smile. "My only real friend was, and still is, Charisse. As for my family," she hesitated, then sighed deeply, "they're good people—basically. They just never really believed in me."

This was a concept that Sean could not comprehend. Although he was from a poor family, with a mother who raised three boys alone, she always believed, and told him he could do anything he set his mind to. And he never for a second believed differently.

"Why? How on earth could your parents not believe in you?"

"They thought I should be a school teacher or a nurse. My choice of careers was always the topic of heated discussions at the dinner table." She gave a wry smile at the recollection. "They just felt that it was a male profession and I had no business sticking my nose in it.'"

"Well, I'm glad you did." Then he added gently, placing his hand on hers, "Otherwise, I may have never met you." His voice and eyes held her captive for just a heartbeat, before she broke the tenuous connection.

"As for old boyfriends—" a tight knot formed in her stomach, "they were few and far between. And on that note, I'd say, let's get the check. It's getting late."

Sean raised his hand to catch the waitress' attention, but his eyes never left Khendra's face. There was a haunted, lonely look hovering in her eyes. A pain that was just beginning to heal. What had happened to her to suppress the vibrancy he knew she had within? What had made her so cautious and leery? Hurt was an emo-

tion he was totally familiar with, and he had learned how to tackle it and become the victor. If she'd only give him a chance, he could teach her to forget.

"Ready?" she asked, breaking into his thoughts.

"I'm with the driver," he answered with a smile.

When they returned to the garage, the rain had slackened somewhat, but rolls of thunder still punctuated the heavens. The air remained heavy with moisture and foreboding. Khendra pulled her car up next to Sean's.

"I guess this is my stop," Sean said halfheartedly. He turned to her. She froze, gripping the steering wheel with all of her strength. She wouldn't look at him. The safe ambiguity and momentary fantasy of the restaurant was gone. She no longer had the security of a public place. Now it was she and him—alone. Suddenly, she wished that he would leave—now. The evening was over, wasn't it?

"Was our dinner as bad as you thought it would be?" he asked gently.

She suddenly felt overheated. "Bad? No...it was really nice. I had a great time." *Oh, please get out.* Her stomach lurched and twisted into a tiny ball.

"Maybe we could do it again...like Friday night." He turned toward her, but she stared straight ahead.

"I don't think that's such a good idea." She

scrambled for a reason. "I...I don't make a habit of going out with members of the firm," she added quickly.

"I think it would be a great idea," he said, his smooth voice working its way through her nervous system. "Every rule has an exception, Khendra, even your rules."

She whipped her head toward him, ready to snap out a hasty reply, but was stopped cold by the depth of intensity that burned in his ebony eyes. She couldn't breathe.

"Good night," he said softly. He leaned forward and gently brushed a kiss across her forehead.

The slight tickle of his mustache sent shivers down her spine. But before she could take her next breath, he was out of her car and moving behind the wheel of his own. She heard the rev of the engine, and saw the headlights blaze across the concrete. Not once did she move. Never once did he look back. The spot he had kissed still burned like fire, even as she turned to watch the taillights of his car disappear down the tunnel.

≈≋≈

As she looked out onto the city from her terrace, hot, humid air blew caressingly through Khendra's thin, pale pink nightgown. A single drop of perspiration threaded its way down between her breasts, a poignant reminder of how lonely she was and how much she'd truly love the feel of a caring hand to wipe that drop away.

With that thought, a vision of Sean bloomed before her eyes, and she felt a slow, steady warming start in the pit of her stomach and radiate downward to her center. She tried to imagine the feel of his powerful hands stroking the hidden places, the feel of his lips against her own. She breathed in deeply the fragrant, rain-washed air, and shook her head to clear the vision.

Chapter Four

For the next three days, Khendra made it a point to stay as far away from Sean Michaels as she could. Her workload made it easy. Every working hour was spent in the courtroom. The only time she saw him, since their evening together, was at the daily morning briefings or when they passed in the corridors. He was pleasant, but cool, almost as if nothing had transpired between them. It was fine with her, she convinced herself. He had almost entered that hidden place she had closed off, and she couldn't let that happen—even though his dreamy voice and carefree laughter floated to her ears and rushed through her veins when she least expected it. But she would put Sean Michaels out of her mind, if it was the last thing she did.

Early Friday morning, as she hovered over her desk preparing her closing argument, she received an unannounced visit. The light knock on her office door broke into her concentration.

"I see you're busy, as usual." Her head snapped up at the interruption to see Alex framed in the doorway. She had wrestled with the offer he'd made for the past three days and, after much cajoling from Charisse, she'd made her decision.

"Please come in, Mr. Counts," she said smoothly. "I was just completing my closing statement for this afternoon."

He strolled into the office and stubbed out a cigarette in the never-used ashtray sitting on her credenza. Khendra instinctively turned up her nose.

"Have you come to a decision?" he asked, cutting through any small talk.

"Yes, I have." She slipped off her glasses and placed them and her gold pen down on the cluttered desk. "I've decided to accept. If the offer is still open."

A pleased smile spread across Alex's face. "A very wise decision. You won't regret it. I hope," he added, his look cutting right through her, "I won't regret it either. I'm putting a lot on the line for you." His voice dropped an octave. "I'm sure you'll show your appreciation."

A wave of apprehension flooded through her. She rose from her seat and looked at him without flinching a muscle, her voice firm and decisive. "I'm an attorney, first and foremost, Mr. Counts. You hired me to do a job and I intend to do it. I hope that answers any questions you may have."

A chuckle rose from his throat. "But you're also a woman, Khendra. A very ambitious, intelligent and beautiful woman. Don't forget that when you're winding your way to the top." With that, he turned and walked out of the office.

Khendra braced her palms against the desk and lowered her head. The only sound in the office was her rapid breathing. She slammed the desk drawer shut and paced the room. This time the insinuation was clear. He expected more from her than just a hard day's work in payment for getting her a partnership with the firm. She had hoped she was wrong, but it was obvious now that she wasn't.

She rubbed her forehead as if to erase the troubled thoughts that tramped through her brain. She had to find a way to combat him without losing her very precarious position. She needed time to think, but now wasn't the time, with less than two hours left to complete her statement before the afternoon session began. A man's future rested in her hands. Her strategy for handling Alex Counts would have to wait.

≈≈

"...ladies and gentlemen, you've heard the district attorney accuse my client, Earl Holmes," she turned to him for emphasis, "of a most heinous crime. Even I was sickened by the depravity of the act." Khendra's voice rose to a thundering pitch as she paced back and forth in front of the jury. "However, not once, I repeat, not once, has the state been able to prove that Earl Holmes, father, husband, laborer, committed this act of violence. All of the state's evidence has been superficial at best. There is no physical evidence what-soever linking my client to this crime." She slapped her hand down on the railing to hammer home her point.

The few nods from the jury gave Khendra the encouraging spark she needed. She lowered her voice to a threadbare whisper, forcing the jurors to strain to catch her every word.

"Yes, something terrible happened on the night of November third. A store owner was brutally, thoughtlessly murdered. His wife is a widow and his children are fatherless. The community is outraged. Someone must pay." She faced the jury, her eyes burn-ing through each and every one of them. "But that someone is not in this room, and to me, that is more frightening, because the real murderer is still out there among us—"

Sean sat in the back of the courtroom, mesmer-ized by the power, authority and magic Khendra wield-ed upon the jurors. The passion with which she spoke brought a new dignity to the profession. She seemed to

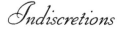

grab those jurors by the gut, refusing to let go until they had absorbed her words, felt them, believed them.

Seeing her in the arena in which she was certainly a master, he discovered a new respect for her. He wondered, as he made a silent exit from the courtroom, if she would ever allow him to incite that kind of passion in her. He knew, deep down in his bones, that given half a chance, together they could reach heights that neither had dreamed possible.

Not even the pressures of a new career seemed as challenging as the elusive Khendra Phillips. But he'd never backed off from a challenge. Yes, he would go after her with the same vigor he went after every thing he wanted in his life. She seemed to have awakened something dark and sensual in his soul, a feeling long forgotten. There could be no casual liaison with Khendra. No, she was a woman who would demand and deserve more. Was he up to the challenge? At the moment, with a promising future stretched out before him, he was certain he could handle anything. Even Khendra.

Chapter Five

Khendra half-walked, half-dragged herself to her front door. It had been an unbelievable week, the likes of which she couldn't recall experiencing before. Her one comfort was the jury had voted unanimously to acquit her client of all charges.

In a matter of days, radical changes had taken place in her life. Her usual orderly world was still vibrating from the aftermath. Not only had her career taken on new dimensions, so had her private life. Her dinner with Sean had somehow given her a different perspective about him, and forced her to take a hard look at her life.

In the days since that evening, she had tried unsuccessfully to exorcise him from her mind. All the reasons she used to justify disliking him fell short. He wasn't the person she thought he would be. He was gentle, warm, sensual and considerate. He seemed interested in her as a person, not a thing to flaunt or try to use to get ahead, as she had suspected. She also realized that she was disappointed that he hadn't mentioned again his offer of another dinner date. Then again, she thought as she shifted her bag of groceries to her hip and dug in her purse for her keys, she hadn't given him any reason to think he had a chance with her.

She pushed the door open, went straight to the kitchen, and deposited the heavy load on the counter. She walked back to the living room with an ice-cold can of Coke in her hand, kicked off her shoes and tossed her jacket on the sofa. Flopping down on the sofa, she popped the top and took a quick, cooling swallow of the Coke, as she reached over to the end table and pressed the button on her answering machine. After a series of beeps, the last voice she expected to hear floated to her ears.

"Hi, it's Sean. I guess you didn't expect to hear from me, since you didn't give me your number. I checked with Phyllis in Personnel and charmed it out of her. I hope you're not angry. I just wanted to tell you I had a wonderful time the other night, and I didn't forget about dinner. I just figured you'd say no. I don't handle rejection very well. It took me all this time to get my courage up. Anyway, I still want to see you— tomorrow, if you're free. I'm going to the racquetball court in the back of the health club on Peachtree Street.

I'll be there from about two o'clock until closing. If you decide you want to see me as much as I'd like to see you, stop by. Hopefully, we can make an evening of it."

She replayed the tape, letting Sean's satiny voice glide through her head. Following Sean's message, there was a message from Charisse about a party, but Khendra couldn't concentrate. Hugging herself in delight, she leaned back on the sofa and shut off the machine, never even listening to Charisse's bubbly voice. All she could hear was the pounding of her heart.

The evening did mean something to him, she thought, elated. He still wanted to see her. Then her moment of joy was quashed when clouds of doubt filtered to the forefront. If she went to the club, he would probably feel real smug and pleased with himself, and she'd feel like a fool. If she didn't go, she might blow a great chance with the first man she'd been attracted to since Tony. She couldn't think straight. Maybe a hot shower and a good night's sleep would clear her mind. But first she would give Charisse a call and get her opinion. She quickly dialed her number. Charisse answered on the first ring.

"...so are you going to meet him or not?"

"I don't think I should. He'll just think I'm running after him."

"Don't be ridiculous. This is the nineties. If he went to the trouble of convincing hard-ass Phyllis to give him your number, it's not because he wants you to chase after him. Wake up, girl!"

"Maybe you're right," Khendra smiled, her spirits lifting. "But I'm just so afraid, Cee Cee. What if I get involved? What if I fall in love? What if he hurts me?"

"Whoa! What's with all the what-ifs? Why can't you just take it for what it's worth, just one day at a time? Trust your instincts, Khen. Besides, you play a mean game of racquetball. You'll probably whip his tail, anyway. That ought to be some consolation. Matter of fact, I'm not doin' a thing tomorrow. If it'll make you feel better, I'll tag along."

"Would you?" Khendra's voice filled with relief.

"Of course, ya big baby. What kinda friend do you think I am?"

"You're a doll, Charisse."

"Yeah, I know."

≈≈≈

The next morning, Khendra was up with the sun. The combination of excitement and jangling nerves had her adrenaline pumping. She had to burn off some of the excess energy. She scrubbed her face, brushed her teeth and pulled on a pair of neon-yellow shorts and a matching tee shirt. She hunted through her closet and

found her running sneakers, and went jogging for an hour.

By noon, she had vacuumed her entire apartment, washed two loads of laundry, changed the linen on her bed, cleaned the oven, and watered all the plants on the terrace. Room by room, she took inventory of her uniquely-designed apartment. Her large bedroom, which opened onto a balcony, was immaculate. The white, freshly hung curtains and matching bedspread contrasted nicely with the lavender walls and carpet. Crossing the foyer, she entered the living room. The smoked-glass wall unit sparkled. She turned on the cabinet lights to showcase the various African sculptures that were strategically displayed on the shelves. The glass coffee table and end tables didn't have a smudge on them. And her newly-purchased crystal vase held freshly-cut flowers, their scent filling the room.

Khendra placed her hands on her hips and took a deep breath. There was nothing left to do but take a shower, get dressed and wait. She crossed the short distance from her living room to the kitchen and searched the well-stocked refrigerator for something cool to drink. She pulled out a large bottle of cranberry juice and took a glass from an overhead cabinet.

Sitting at her round butcher block table sipping her glass of juice, Khendra wondered what her afternoon with Sean would be like. She was glad Charisse was going with her. At least she wouldn't feel so awkward. Then her heart skipped a beat when she visualized Sean's face and how he must look in a pair of shorts. A quiver of excitement ran up her spine at the vision and she quickly shook it away. She was getting way ahead of herself She was just going to play an innocent game of racquetball.

As she sat there convincing herself that meeting Sean was perfectly aboveboard, she was interrupted by the ringing of the phone.

"Hello?"

"Khendra. I'm glad I caught you at home. This is Alex Counts."

Khendra's brows knitted into a frown. "Yes, Mr. Counts. Is something wrong?" She tried to keep the uneasy feeling out of her voice.

"No, nothing at all. Actually, I was calling to see if you were free this afternoon. I was going to send a car around to pick you up and bring you out to my boat. I'm having a few close friends over for drinks."

Oh, no. Just what I don't need. "Well, actually, Mr. Counts, I do have plans," she answered as calmly as she could. "And I don't drink," she added, hoping to lend strength to her response.

She heard him clear his throat and several seconds passed before he spoke. "I see. This was rather short notice. Next time I'll be sure to give you plenty of advance notice."

Next time! "I usually try to keep myself pretty busy on the weekends," she lied.

"I'm sure that even with your busy schedule, you take time out for dinner." The statement hung suggestively in the air.

"Of course, but—"

"Then we'll have dinner. One night soon. Have a lovely day, Khendra. I'll see you on Monday."

Before she had a chance to respond, he hung up the phone.

"Damn!" She slammed the phone down on the cradle and threaded her free hand through her hair. She was going to have to find a way to put a stop to this, and soon. She began pacing the floor, sucking on her thumbnail as she walked. She had heard the rumors about Alex Counts, but never in her wildest dreams would she have thought he'd be interested in her. Maybe it was a mistake to take his offer, especially with the subtle innuendoes attached. No! She deserved the partnership, and she would get it without jumping into bed with Alex Counts!

Taking a final swallow from her glass of juice, she walked over to the phone and turned off the answering machine. If he decided to call again, he would get no response. She then began stripping her clothes off, as she ridded herself of the ugly feeling Alex had stirred up in her, and headed for the shower.

Freshly showered, and clad only in a bath towel, she searched through the chest at the foot of her bed for the perfect outfit. Suddenly, her feminine instincts had rushed to the forefront and it became significantly important what Sean saw and felt when he looked at her. Finally, she decided on hot pink, terry shorts and a pink cotton tank top with white ribbing down the sides. She sat on the bed and pulled on pink sweat socks, then put on her favorite pair of white sneakers. Fully clothed, she stood in front of the bathroom mirror. Taking a hard bristle brush, she vigorously ran it through her thick hair until it shone. Then she took an ivory barrette and pulled the mass of hair into a ponytail. Smiling with satisfaction, she gave her hair a final pat, then brushed her lips with a hint of mahogany-colored lip gloss.

With about twenty minutes left before Charisse was due to arrive, she sat on the sofa and flipped through a current issue of the Atlanta Sun Times. There was a large spread on page three about the abortion clinic bombing, heralding Sean's legal maneuvers in the courtroom. Next to the article was a full-length picture of Sean standing on the courthouse steps.

A pang of irrational jealousy swept through her as she gazed upon the unquestionably handsome, smiling face. It took all of her self-control to restrain the resentment she still felt about the case. The one consolation was that she'd at least attempted to put Sean in perspective. She couldn't hold him responsible, and hopefully they wouldn't be pitted against each other again. What was done, was done. She also realized that in order for anything to work between her and Sean, she would have to be up front with him about her feelings. Maybe today would be the day.

Sighing, she tossed the paper back on the coffee table, rose from the sofa and walked toward the terrace. The cloudless sky promised a glorious day. Lush, stately trees dotted the pavement and fragrant flowers graced the well-tended gardens. Khendra leaned against the wrought-iron railing and deeply breathed in the fragrant air, which brought back recollections of the last time she stood in the very same spot. The thought made her heart quicken.

This time her meeting with Sean was planned. She was taking a planned risk, something she only felt comfortable doing in the courtroom. But strangely enough, she was beginning to feel good about it. The anxiety was making way for excitement.

Turning back inside, she slid the glass doors shut, just as the doorbell rang. Khendra checked her watch, a puzzled look creasing her brow. Who in the world could that be? It couldn't be Charisse, she concluded with certainty. She was rarely on time, and definitely never early. She walked to the door and stole a quick look through the peephole. Her breath caught in her throat, and her hand flew to her mouth to stifle the gasp that slipped through her lips. She took a calming breath and swallowed hard, commanding herself to breathe in and out. The door bell rang again, jarring her into action. She swung the door open and faced her unexpected guest with a defiant stance. "Mr. Counts, what an unexpected surprise."

Chapter Six

"May I come in?" Before the words were halfway out of his mouth, he had stepped over the threshold and was candidly assessing her apartment.

"Nice place. You have excellent taste." He turned to face her.

Khendra didn't move, but spoke from the open doorway. "What are you doing here, Mr. Counts?" She tried to camouflage the indignation that tinged her voice. "I'm sure I explained to you that I have plans for today."

"Yes, I don't doubt that you do," he said, his blue eyes raking over her long, shapely legs. He walked slowly toward the terrace. Turning, he added, "However, I felt that a personal invitation would help sway your decision."

"I'm sorry you came all this way for nothing. Anyway," she added, her temper rising, "I fail to see how accepting an invitation to go sailing with you has anything to do with my job."

He began to move toward her. "It has every-thing to do with your job." His voice became menacing as he continued. "And the sooner you recognize these invitations as little stepping stones, the sooner you'll get to the top."

She felt her breath quickening as he drew near-er. Where was Charisse? "Stepping stones to the top, for me, means only hard work and dedication," she said evenly. "Now I really appreciate your stopping by, Mr. Counts, but I'm expecting my friend any moment now, and I still have a few things to do." She prayed he did-n't hear the tremor she felt in her voice.

He moved into the open doorway. Khendra braced herself. He raised his index finger and trailed it down the small cleft in her chin. She immediately pulled back. Her eyes blazed with outrage. She opened her mouth to speak, but Alex cut her off.

"I know what you're thinking," he said in a low voice. "You'll report all of this to the board." He chuckled, but his eyes held no humor. "Who would believe you? You'd only end up hurting yourself in the long run. Remember, my favors can be very valuable, Khendra."

"I want you to—"

"Hey, girl, you ready?" Charisse said, appearing

as if on cue. She looked from one to the other. "Something wrong?" She eased her way in between Alex and Khendra, which forced Alex to take a retreating step.

Khendra had never been so happy to see anyone in her life. Intense relief flooded through her taut body. "No. Mr. Counts was just leaving."

"Is this *the* Mr. Counts?"

"Yes." Khendra clenched her jaw. "Charisse Carter, this is Alex Counts, one of the senior partners at the firm."

He turned to Charisse and flashed a smile. He extended a tanned hand, which she took. "It's a pleasure to meet you, Ms. Carter. Perhaps we'll have a chance to meet again." He turned back to Khendra. "I hope you'll think about what I said." He nodded his goodbye to Charisse and walked toward the elevator.

"What in the hell did I just walk in on?" Charisse stepped into the apartment, tossed her bag on a chair and turned to Khendra. What she saw made her rush back to Khendra's side. "You're shaking all over." Her eyes whipped around the room for any signs of disturbance. "What the devil did he say to you? What did he do?" She put an arm around Khendra, closed the door and ushered her into the living room.

Once she was seated, Khendra felt her heartbeat slowly return to normal. Charisse kept a protective arm around her until some of the trembling stopped.

"You just sit right there," Charisse commanded, pointing a warning finger. She entered the kitchen and searched through the refrigerator and cabinets. "Don't you have anything stronger to drink in here besides cranberry juice?" she called over her shoulder.

"You know I don't drink," Khendra mumbled. "There's some Coke on the bottom shelf."

Charisse grabbed a glass, loaded it with ice and poured the fizzling coke over the cubes. Returning to the sofa, she pushed the glass into Khendra's trembling fingers. "Drink this," she ordered." She stood over her, watched Khendra's shaky hands bring the glass to her lips, and waited until she had drank the last drop. "You feel like talking now?"

Khendra nodded her head. Slowly, she began with the veiled comments Alex had made at the office, and led up to his visit to her apartment.

"Why didn't you tell me about this before?" Charisse demanded, furious at Khendra.

"I had hoped I was mistaken, and I thought you'd think I was overreacting again." She looked up guiltily at Charisse, who just shook her head.

"You should know better than that, girl.

Especially when it comes to something like this. Did he threaten you? Did he put his hands on you?"

Khendra rose from the sofa and began pacing back and forth, her long, slender fingers dramatizing her words. "It wasn't so much what he said, Cee Cee, it was how he said it and what it implied. If you hadn't walked in when you did, I don't know what he may have tried."

"I'm sure he's not a stupid man, Khen. He's choosing his words very carefully. That's why he's so sure you won't say anything. It would be your word against his. And if you take it at face value, he's actually said nothing or done anything that's threatening.'"

"I know. That's what's so frustrating and what makes me so damned angry." She stomped her foot and turned pleading eyes on Charisse. "I have to find a way to deal with him. This is all very touchy. If I say or do the wrong thing, I could be ruined. I'm finally beginning to understand how innocent people are painted as bad guys."

Charisse sighed. "You just have to stand your ground. He wouldn't dare try anything at the office, and just don't let yourself be alone with him. You don't have anything on him unless he tries something."

"I know," she replied resignedly.

"Well, you know what you have to work with. In the meantime, I'd just say the hell with him."

"You're right. I shouldn't let him shake me up

like this. It was just that I felt so trapped. The way he looked at me." She wrapped her arms protectively around her body.

Charisse got up and stood beside her. "You're getting yourself all worked up again. Let's get out of here, so you can take out some of that hostility on the court. Anyway, I'm dying to see the man that finally plucked those rusty heartstrings."

Khendra's face softened in a smile of gratitude, as she embraced Charisse in a warm hug. Then, holding her at arm's length, she asked, "What would I do without you?"

"Is that a trick question?" Charisse teased, twisting her face in mock confusion.

"Come on, you," Khendra said, grabbing her small duffel bag and giving Charisse a playful shove. "Let's get out of here."

Sean stood in a phone booth at the corner of Dr. Martin Luther King, Jr. Drive, listening to the hollow ringing of the phone on the other end. He checked his watch. It was already two-thirty. His heart sank. She wouldn't wait, he just knew it. He helplessly watched the steam rise from the hood of his car, and looked at the twisted metal of the car that had cut him off.

Chapter Seven

Khendra sat on the long, wooden bench and looked up at the huge wall clock. They had been at the club for nearly two hours. "He's not coming, Cee Cee," she said finally. "This was probably just a tactic to make me feel like an idiot, and it worked. I knew I shouldn't—"

"Come on Khen, maybe something happened," Charisse reassured her, no longer sure she believed it herself.

"Sure," Khendra sighed in disgust, trying to hide her bruised pride. "Come on, I'm not going to stay any longer. If he does show up, which I doubt, he won't find me here waiting with bated breath."

She grabbed her bag, marched down the carpeted corridor and out the glass doors. Charisse followed close behind, feeling almost as bad as her friend. Khendra had been so reluctant to involve herself with anyone. Now, when she finally takes a chance again, she gets humiliated. Charisse wanted to ring Sean's neck herself, but she had to keep her own spirits up for Khendra's sake.

As the doors swung shut behind them, the pert receptionist flipped on the microphone. "Would Ms. Khendra Phillips please come to the front desk. You have a phone call. Ms. Phillips—"

Khendra slunk back into the passenger seat of Charisse's Mustang, feeling completely humiliated, as Charisse gunned the engine and drove out of the parking lot.

Sean stood in a phone booth just off the main road, feeling the minutes and Khendra slip away, as his page for her remained unanswered.

≈≫

A warm, early evening breeze gently stroked the patrons of the outdoor cafe. Khendra absently picked at her plate of shrimp and rice, the sting of Sean's stunt lingering behind her dark brown eyes. She should have trusted her instincts. He was no different from any of the other men who had tried to ease their way into her life. And to think she had been willing to give him a chance. What a fool she was.

Charisse watched the array of emotions flit

across Khendra's liquid gold face. She had to find a way to snap her out of her dismal mood. Especially since she felt partially responsible.

"Listen, why don't we drive downtown, do some shopping and then crash at my house? I haven't been on a wild shopping spree in ages, and I feel daring," she said with as much gaiety as she could summon.

"No. I really don't feel like shopping," she mumbled.

"Well, you ain't gonna sit around sulking all day. And anyway, I'm driving." She dangled the car keys tauntingly in the air.

Khendra sighed in resignation. "All right. I give up. Let's go shopping."

"A woman after my own heart. Just point me in the right direction." Charisse draped her arm across Khendra's stiff shoulders. This was going to take a lot of shopping.

❧

Sean hung up his phone for the last time. He had called Khendra's apartment through Saturday evening, all day Sunday and well into Sunday night. It was becoming obvious that she wasn't coming home, or worse, she didn't want to talk to him.

He put his bare feet up on the sofa and leaned

back into the cottony softness, furious with himself. If he hadn't been so wrapped up in that damned case, he would have left his apartment in plenty of time and would not have been racing down the highway. But who was to say she even showed up? *She probably didn't*, he consoled himself. But if she did, he'd just explain everything tomorrow. She seemed like a reasonable woman and he felt confident she would accept his explanation.

Fortifying himself with that thought, he closed his dark eyes and drifted off to sleep, with visions of Khendra dancing through his mind.

Late Sunday evening, Khendra returned to her apartment totally exhausted. Kicking off her shoes and dropping her shopping bag of new clothes in the foyer, she headed straight for her bedroom. Within minutes, she had slipped out of her clothes, showered and crawled into bed.

As she lay staring up at the stuccoed ceiling, she realized with a twinge of apprehension that it was the first time since Saturday morning she had been alone with her thoughts, and that sinking sensation rapidly returned.

How could she have been so gullible as to think

that Sean really cared about her? He was probably used to women who just dropped at his feet, and expected her to do the same. She had promised herself she would give him the benefit of the doubt, against her better judgment. He had proven royally that he didn't deserve it.

Turning on her side, she struggled into a fitful sleep. Her last conscious thought was that she was completely miserable.

❦

"As you all know," began Alex, "Mr. McMahon will be leaving us in a few short months. Therefore, the position of junior partner will be open once Mr. McMahon's position is filled by the very capable, Darren Kennedy."

A short round of applause echoed throughout the room.

"As a senior partner of this firm, I have made my own recommendations." His magnetic blue eyes moved slowly around the conference table and lit, briefly, on Khendra. She quickly looked away.

"However," he continued, "any one of you who feels he or she has the capabilities to fill this position may submit a proposal in writing. Based on a review of these proposals, the principals will make a determination." With that statement, he turned to the attorney seated next to him .

"Now as that was the final issue of the morning, intoned the stately Gordon Perry, picking up his cue, "This meeting is adjourned."

The half-dozen attorneys began to rise, whispering among themselves about the possibilities. All of them knew that whoever Alex had recommended was virtually guaranteed the spot.

Khendra quickly gathered up her notes and draped her maroon linen blazer over her arm, just as one of the associates sidled up to her.

"Tough break about the clinic case," Brendan Clarke gave her a cynical grin. "Looks like you've been demoted." He angled his head in Sean's direction. "Better luck next time." He patted her on the shoulder and walked out.

Using all the self-control she could muster, she bit her tongue. She wasn't going to let the remarks get to her, she vowed again. She was sure Brendan's comments wouldn't be the last.

The main thing she had on her mind at the moment was getting out of the room before Sean said anything to her. As she looked up, she saw him conclude his conversation with one of the attorneys and begin to move in her direction. Quickly, she stuffed her notebook in her briefcase and turned toward the door.

"Khendra." The black satin voice shimmied down her spine.

For a split second she considered stopping, but her instincts propelled her forward. She heard his rapid, muffled footsteps close in behind her as she quickly strutted down the corridor. Just as she approached the threshold of her office door, his large hand braced her shoulder.

"You're still running from me."

She whirled around to face him, hurt and humiliation rimming her eyelids. But when she looked into those magical midnight eyes, the torrid words she wanted to lash out at him caught in her throat. For a brief moment, she nearly forgot why she was so angry. Then sanity returned.

"Please let go of me, Mr. Michaels," she said, as coldly as she could. She looked at his hand as if it had grown claws.

"So...now we're back to Mister. Is that it?" He reluctantly removed his hand, the tingling sensation from the brief contact still racing up and down his arm.

"Look," she said, venom rising in her voice, "you seem to be an expert at deception, and I don't have time to play your little games."

He visibly winced from the sting of her words, and Khendra immediately felt a surge of satisfaction.

"I know I owe you an explanation. If you'll—"

"You don't owe me anything, Mr. Michaels. If it doesn't have to do with business, we have nothing to discuss." She turned and walked into her office, slamming the door in his face.

Sean stood on the other side of the closed door in temporary disbelief. Then his own anger boiled to the surface. Who the hell did she think she was anyway? He didn't have to take that from anyone. He stormed into his own office, slamming the door solidly behind him.

Still fuming, he flung himself into his chair and spun toward the window, a deep frown creasing his brow. It wasn't often that he wore his emotions on his sleeve. Now when he did, he gets smacked square in the face.

What was worse, the insult was coming from someone who obviously didn't give a damn about him in the first place. His ebony eyes cut across the horizon in disgust.

Then a flash of insight hit him. She did care! Why else would she have been so upset? *Women!* He should have seen that. He took a deep, relieved breath. Turning to face his desk, a slow smile of understanding spread across his lips. He would just have to handle Ms. Phillips with kid gloves, he realized. She was certainly not going to stand still for any excuses, and he had to be sure not to give her any. At that moment, he was more

determined than ever to have her in his life, and he
would not allow her icy front to dissuade him.

He briefly glanced up at the grandfather clock
standing in the far corner of the spacious office, and his
mind turned to the business at hand. In less than an
hour, he was due in court. This case was really taking
its toll on him. The press had hounded him from the
first day. There wasn't a day since the jury selection
began that he hadn't been photographed, questioned or
misquoted. Well, if he wanted notoriety, he certainly
had it with this case. The district attorney's office was
watching his every move.

He gathered up his notes and prepared to leave.
Then, just as he reached the door, an idea struck him.
The perfect touch, he thought, a boyish light filling his
eyes. He walked back to the phone and dialed information.

Chapter Eight

The brilliance of the setting sun cast orange and gold hues across the skyline. The light appeared to dance off the glass window, highlighting it in a rainbow of effervescent color.

Rising from behind her desk, Khendra stretched her tight muscles and strolled toward the window. Her luminous eyes spanned the horizon, allowing the magnificence of the evening to soothe her harried spirit. With the day finally drawing to a close, she knew she could no longer put aside the issues that were wreaking havoc with her thoughts. She had successfully avoided Sean and Alex all day, but she could not hibernate in her office forever. Turning away from the window, she prepared to leave, when there was a light knock at the door.

"Come in."

Leslie came through the door, her arms laden with a huge arrangement of roses. Khendra's eyes widened in surprise.

"These just arrived for you, Ms. Phillips." She gingerly placed the flowers on the wide window sill.

"Who on earth could these be from?" Khendra asked, more to herself than to Leslie.

"There's a card," Leslie offered, her own curiosity peaked. Khendra was labeled "the ice lady" throughout the office. She had turned down every request for a date in the past three years, so to see her receive flowers made Leslie feel warm inside. Deep down she knew that Khendra was one of the nicest people around. She was just glad to know that someone else thought the same thing.

Khendra reached for the card and silently read the scrawled inscription. "I'm sorry. I hope you'll give me a chance to apologize."

Khendra's heart filled to near bursting. A warm smile formed on her lips.

"Anyone interesting?"

Khendra looked up and smiled. "Quite," she said softly, a faraway look in her eyes. She took a shaky breath. "Well...it's getting late. I'd better be going."

Leslie got the hint, and knew that her curiosity would not be satisfied. "See you in the morning, Ms. Phillips."

Khendra didn't hear Leslie's words or see her leave. For countless moments, she reread the words on the card and stared, hypnotically, at the beautiful arrangement of yellow, white and red roses.

He had gone out of his way to apologize. Maybe something did happen to him on Saturday after all. She gently stroked one of the budding roses. Could she have been that wrong? Or was this another one of his ploys? She shook her head in confusion. Well, there was no way of knowing until she spoke with him. This time, if he offered, she would at least listen.

She gathered up her belongings, switched off the lights and headed for the garage.

Sean paced nervously. He checked his watch. She should be down any minute. Then the elevator doors to the garage slowly opened. His muscles tightened when he saw her. It was now or never. But suppose she wouldn't listen? *I'll just have to make you listen. Won't I?*

He waited until she had reached her car and inserted the key in the lock. Quietly, he walked up behind her. "Hi."

She turned, startled, then was immediately relieved. "Do you always sneak up on defenseless women?" she asked coyly, a soft smile outlining her full lips.

Sean's heart raced. "I'm really quite harmless." He moved closer, encouraged by her response. "I've been trying to tell you that."

"You've been trying to tell me a lot of things. I guess I just haven't been listening." She lowered her eyes, then looked up at him, a hopeful light filling the warm pools.

"This may not be the right time to ask for a favor, but could you give me a lift?"

Khendra's eyes rapidly surveyed the garage. "Where's your car?"

"I had a little accident on Saturday, on my way to the club."

Khendra's heart caught in her throat. Haunting images of Tony's lifeless body flashed through her brain, and the ceaseless feelings of guilt rushed to the surface. "Was anyone hurt," she asked in an unsteady voice.

"Only you and me," he said softly, a bit shaken by the look of anguish that darkened her eyes. "I'd like to change all that, if you'll let me."

Khendra's heartbeat slowly returned to normal, as she forced the visions of Tony back into her subconscious.

"I think I have some making up to do myself. How about dinner, at my house?" She startled herself at the spontaneity of her words, but was happy she had made the decision.

"I can't think of anything I'd rather do."

Khendra, too nervous to drive, handed him the keys and walked around to the passenger side of the car. "You drive."

As Sean eased into the car, Khendra's body tensed with the nearness of him.

"I really thought you'd never speak to me again," he said, maneuvering the car around the winding turns.

She took a calming breath before answering. "You were almost right. I have a bad habit of jumping to conclusions."

"I hadn't noticed," he quipped with a teasing smile. "But I dialed your number so many times over the weekend, your phone number was singing to me in my sleep."

"I turned my machine off. Had a problem," she said, somewhat thrilled that he had tried repeatedly to reach her.

"I was sure I was doomed. I didn't think you'd believe me. I even thought of camping out on your doorstep."

"What stopped you?" An amused look danced in her soft brown eyes.

"I knew that if you saw me sprawled there, and just stepped over my body, I would never recover from the humiliation. You do have an air of indifference about you." He turned to her and smiled.

"It's just that it's not often that I—" she hesitated, then shrugged her shoulders.

"Get involved?" he said, completing her sentence.

"Something like that." She lowered her eyes.

"That's going to change," he said assuredly. Khendra's heart skipped a fraction of a beat. "I can guarantee it."

≈⊛≈

"You're not only beautiful and intelligent, you're, a great cook," Sean said as he took the last mouth-watering forkful of steamed red snapper and sautéed rice and washed it down with a long swallow of sparkling cider.

"I'm glad you enjoyed it, sir." She gave a mock bow as she rose to clear the table.

"Let me help you with those." Sean collected the glasses and silverware and followed her into the kitchen.

He never ceases to amaze me, Khendra thought, as she filled the sink with hot, sudsy water. He didn't appear to be the type of man who would be handy in the kitchen, or even want to be associated with one. His somewhat arrogant exterior belied the caring man underneath. Khendra's heart smiled at the revelation and wondered in anticipation what other surprises Sean Michaels had up his sleeve.

They worked in companionable silence, the misunderstanding of the weekend having been explained and put behind them. The only sounds were the rushing water, and the soft beat of the stereo as Anita Baker's throaty alto voice embraced them with her hit, Rapture.

The intimacy of the moment, the good food and soft music, intensified in the sultry atmosphere. Intermittently, their fingers brushed each other's, and with each contact electricity charged the air.

Khendra's heart beat erratically in her chest, while Sean tried valiantly to control the mounting desire he felt for this tantalizing woman. He turned to her. She held her breath. He slowly reached over and wiped away a spot of soapy water from the cleft in her chin. The brief contact sent rivers of fire rushing through her veins.

Sean searched her eyes as if wanting to enter her soul. Then, before she knew what happened, he lowered his head and gently brushed her lips with his own. He instantly felt powerless to control the surge of emotion that flooded his being, and without thinking any further, he pulled her possessively into his arms, his mouth locking with hers.

Khendra felt her spirit leave her body as she gave in to the delight of their first kiss. Slowly, she lifted her arms and wrapped them around his neck, pulling him closer. Primitive, dark, and erotic feelings soared through her with the nearness of him. She could feel every muscle, every fiber of his being as he pressed urgently against her, filling all the dips and curves of her body with his own.

His strong, large hands stroked her waist, then her hips, pulling her even closer. A soft moan of raw pleasure slipped through her lips as Sean's expert fingers trailed up and down her spine. He ran his fingers through her thick, auburn hair, as he slid his velvety tongue into her waiting mouth.

An uncontrollable tremor raced through her body, as the heated fluids of arousal filled her to near bursting. Her mind swept through an array of conflicting emotions—desire, longing and fear. Was this what she really wanted? Hidden doubts crept through her brain, like miniature thieves in the night. But the flame of indecision was quickly extinguished when Sean lifted his head and his smoldering gaze bored through her. In that instant, a silent agreement was made. She realized that their relationship was on the brink of taking on a new dimension, and her pulse quickened in expectation. He took her hand and led her out of the room.

Khendra reached for the door to her bedroom,

but Sean gently pulled her in the opposite direction.

"But Sean, I—"

"Ssh. Come with me."

He led her into the bathroom, closed the door and turned on the shower. Khendra stood silently in wide-eyed wonder, as the room quickly filled with steam.

Sean moved toward her, an untamed light filling his eyes. He pulled her to him, and his hot, moist lips smothered her own.

"I want you," he groaned in her ear, his tempting tongue taunting the cord of her neck. He slipped his hands under her white silk blouse, and threaded his fingers through the clasp of her black lace bra. Her swollen breasts seemed to cry out in release, as their heaviness was cupped and kneaded with tender, loving hands.

Khendra tossed her head back in surrender, as in one smooth motion, Sean pushed up her blouse, tempering his hunger on the succulent fruits. The contact was explosive. Sean visibly trembled, while Khendra's breathing escalated into rapid, panting gasps. She wanted to scream, but then his mouth captured hers again.

His hands skillfully slid down her back and unzipped her skirt, letting it fall around her bare feet. Dizzy with a desire she thought was long buried, she began to unbutton his shirt, and loosened the button of his slacks. Her slender fingers traced the outline of his broad, muscular chest, while his hands eased around the elastic of her black slip, and it, too, fell to the floor. Then, raising her arms above her head, Sean removed the sleeveless blouse and pulled her solidly against him, his own blooming desire hard and demanding.

The steam from the shower enveloped them, covering their near-bare bodies in a fine mist. Khendra's hair hung loosely around her shoulders, and Sean reached down to sweep a wispy tendril from her face. Then he caught the look of doubt and confusion clouding her eyes. He stroked her face.

"What is it?" he asked, his throaty voice filled with concern.

"It's been so long...and I don't have...I mean I'm not using—"

The light of understanding quickly filled his eyes. Without another word, he reached for the wallet in his pants pocket and retrieved a small packet, putting her fears to rest. He bent down and lightly kissed the soft smile that tipped her lips. Then reaching for the shower door, he opened it, urging her forward with just a look. They both slipped out of the remnants of their clothing, each marveling at the beauty of the other. Their tan and brown bodies, glistening with perspiration from the heat of the shower, resembled bronze statues after a summer's rain. Together they stepped into the shower and closed the door behind them.

The steamy, pulsing water cascaded over them, cleansing them and arousing them with its beat. Sean took the bar of lavender-scented soap and trailed it across her breasts, making the tips rise in perfect unison. Khendra released a gasp of trembling yearning when the trail led down to the hollow of her stomach, and then to the hidden darkness below. She braced herself against the tiled wall as Sean's large hands slowly stirred the soapy lather over her throbbing body and all its hidden places.

She reached for him, uncertain but tender hands quickening the pulse that pumped through his tortured body. He was sure he could no longer contain the raw desire that hovered on the brink of eruption. He lifted her to him, the threshold of fulfillment only a heartbeat away.

"Khendra," he groaned, his lips crushing hers.

She couldn't think, couldn't breathe, the surreal pleasure of him rendering her incapable of anything other than succumbing to the exquisite sensations that ravished her quivering body. She was lost in a world she never knew existed, and she never wanted to return to that place that had held her captive for so long.

Instinctively, she wrapped her long, shapely legs around his narrow waist, pulling him to her, inciting him with her wanton abandon. His powerful arms held her securely, moving her steadily against him. He desperately wanted to bury himself within the pulsing chasm that cried out to him for fulfillment. But he hesitated, knowing that he wanted that irrevocable moment to be total perfection.

Sean opened the shower door and carried her out of the steamy room and across the hall to the moonlit bedroom. Their wet, dripping bodies instantly saturated the satin, lilac-colored sheets, as the brilliant moonlit sky shone down upon their entwined forms, capturing their outline as an artist's sketch on canvas.

Khendra's exotic beauty—her glistening, butter-soft skin, the arch of her large brown eyes, the swell of her dreamy breasts, and the curve of her waist that flared into firm, rounded hips—had Sean transfixed. As if in a trance, he cupped her face in his palms and slowly lowered his lips to her parted mouth. He felt her tremble beneath him as he stroked her luscious thighs, easing them down on either side of his body.

Inch by inch, his hungry mouth trailed downward, his tongue stroking the pulse that pounded in the hollow of her neck. Downward his searing lips traveled to suckle the jutting tips of each breast. Khendra bit back a cry of bittersweet surrender as the shivery thread of desire raced through her body. Her body arched spontaneously, pressing her heaving breasts against his tantalizing tongue. Surely someone must have lit a fire within her, she thought crazily through the haze of her mounting passion. What else could explain the unearthly heat that blazed within her. She clasped his head in her hand, running her fingers across the waves in his hair, willing him closer, begging him for release with soft moans of his name.

For the first time in his life, Sean felt an unparalleled desire to share with this glorious woman the most intimate moment of loving. Slowly, his hands threaded their way down her body, etching into his memory every inch of the satiny skin, until his searching fingers rested upon the moist bud that hardened at his touch.

Khendra's hips rose spasmodically as the incendiary contact jettisoned throughout her body. She buried her face in her pillow to stifle the cries impelled by these unbelievable sensations that held her hostage. Never in her wildest imaginings could she have been prepared for the unbridled explosion that rocketed through her, as Sean's hungry mouth and hands transported her like a jet to far-reaching horizons of pleasure.

White, hot flashes of light filled her eyes. She heard strange sounds, incomprehensible words filling the room. It wasn't until her throat was almost raw that she realized the cries were coming from deep within her. Her body twisted and arched as if it had a mind of its own. She grabbed the sheet in her fists, sure that if she didn't hold on for dear life she would plunge headlong into a world of no return.

Then she felt it. The slow, steady warming threaded its way up from her toes, making her thighs quiver, her stomach quake, her breathing quicken to panting breaths. Any moment now, the long denial would be satisfied, her dizzying ardor relieved. Her head swam as the pressure built to a savage pitch. She wasn't sure how much more she could stand, and then suddenly, without warning, she was filled to near bursting. A fierce and demanding heat climbed steadily upward until she was sure it had torn away her insides. Her eyes flew open and tears glistened her lashes as the briefest instance of pain quickly gave way to the undeniable power of their union.

Slowly, and with gentle care, Sean moved above her, wanting to bury himself within the liquid fire that had him weak and trembling. He searched her face, trailing kisses across her cheeks, her lips, her neck. He wanted to tell her what she was doing to him, but all he could do was rasp out her name over and over in a ragged, breathless voice.

Time seemed to stand still as they traveled to heights neither had ever experienced. Together they found a new rhythm—melodious, sultry, intoxicating and so perfect. Soft sighs, mixed with low moans filled the room, building in intensity with each plunge and

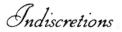
Indiscretions

arch.

Sean gathered Khendra into his arms, his groans muffled in her neck. Quickening his pace, he crushed her lips with his own, mindless of the bruising, knowing only that he wanted to be everywhere within her at once. He didn't want it to end, never wanted this incredible feeling to stop, but he was fast losing ground.

Then in a final moment of desperation, he pulled her on top of him, burying himself deeper within the heated walls, hoping that this would make the dream last forever. But when he looked up into her enchanting face, her eyes half-closed in the throes of passion, her head tossed back in abandon, he knew he could no longer hold back.

He reached up and cupped her full breasts in his palms, kneading the tight, hard nipples between his fingers. She cried out his name as his head arched upward to take a waiting breast into his mouth. Deeper he plunged, forcing Khendra to brace herself on the wooden headboard. Together they raced forward, knowing that they could no longer be denied the sublime pleasure of release.

The evening breeze whipped the sheer white drapes in and out of the open balcony almost in unison with their rhythm, caressing them relentlessly. Sean let out a low groan as the pressure built within him. He grabbed her hips, forcing her to succumb to the urgency that welled inside. Khendra cried out as the spire strained upward. Her breathing was short and erratic, drops of perspiration trailed down her back. This can't be real, she thought as the heat continued to radiate and magnify. Her eyes were misty, her vision blurred as she looked down onto Sean's handsome face. The glorious sensations built to a staggering tempo, the intensity frightening her with its power.

Sean grasped the back of her head in the palm of his hand, his dark eyes scorching through her. He could only grind out a single word through his clenched teeth.

"Now."

He hurled himself upward in deep rapid bursts, pushing her downward with just one large hand. Khendra screamed his name as countless explosions of unsurpassed fulfillment ripped through her, leaving her drained. Sean gathered her in his arms, releasing the last shattering pitch, as he turned her on her back and covered her lips with tender kisses.

Chapter Nine

Khendra lay nestled in Sean's arms, the magnificence of the past few hours clinging to her soul, spinning her heart. She felt overwhelmed by the barrage of emotions that assaulted her. How could she feel so wonderful in this man's arms? Surely she didn't deserve the ecstasy they had experienced.

She snuggled her head against Sean's warm neck, listening intently to his even breathing and the pulse that beat steadily in his throat. She closed her eyes, feeling momentarily content and secure, and was drifting off into a satiated sleep when visions of Tony's boyish face loomed behind her closed lids. His light brown eyes and golden face accused her, and a shiver of guilt ran up her spine.

She squeezed her eyes tighter until tiny sparks of light popped like flashbulbs in her head. Her breathing slowly escalated to tiny, rapid breaths, and a thin film of perspiration covered her body. As if in a dream, she could hear the sound of sirens, high-pitched and chilling. She began to tremble as she saw the flashing red lights, and the sounds of deep hushed voices pounded in her head.

She felt as if she were being swept away into an abyss, the nightmare becoming more real, edging closer with each beat of her heart. Any minute now, the man in the white shirt would say the words. But if she covered her ears, she wouldn't hear them—again.

Then she felt herself being shaken. Someone was calling her name. The voice sounded as if it were coming from a long, dark tunnel. Slowly, the glaring lights and the hushed voices receded and she could just make out a distant light entering the tunnel.

"Khendra! Khendra!"

The voice was getting closer. Suddenly, she jerked upright in the bed, looking frantically around the room. Her whole body was a tight, trembling coil.

"What's wrong? Tell me. What is it?" Sean took her face in his hands, forcing her to look at him.

Then she just seemed to wilt, and Sean gathered her in his arms, pulling her against his pounding heart. He stroked her hair, brushed her forehead with tender kisses, until he felt her breathing return to normal. Gently, he laid her down on the bed, fluffing the pillows behind her. Her large, sad eyes looked up at him as if hoping to find some answer in their inky depths. She took a deep, tremulous breath and slowly closed her eyes.

"I'm sorry," she whispered in a thready voice.

Sean cradled her head against his chest. "You have nothing to worry about. You just scared the hell out of me. That must've been some dream. I never knew I could have such a devastating effect on a woman." He tried a smile to lighten the mood.

Khendra eased out of his embrace and stretched her legs across the edge of the bed. Sean reached for her and she instantly drew away. "Please don't," she pleaded in a strained whisper, standing up and pulling a print kimono around her gentle curves.

"Damn it, Khen. What is it?" He stood up behind her and swung her around to face him. "Talk to me." His deep voice went straight through her, demanding, urgent.

"I...I can't. Not now...not yet." The beginnings of tears christened her eyes.

He pulled her into his arms, feeling his heart thud madly against his chest. Dozens of thoughts swam through his head, but nothing made sense. What transpired between them was more than just sex. It was something he had never experienced before. He knew she felt it too. Then why was she shutting him out, and what had terrified her so? He had gone over the edge this time. He had opened a part of himself that had been closed for too long. And he had no intention of giving up, at least not yet. If she wanted time, he would give it to her—but only for a while.

"All right," he said grudgingly. "If that's the way you want it." He let her go and walked across the hall to the shower.

Moments later, she heard the sounds of rushing water and the earlier, magical images came speeding back. Taking a deep, shaky breath, she pushed the visions away and headed toward the kitchen.

Sean finished showering and put his clothes on. When he came out of the bedroom, he found Khendra sitting at the kitchen table, staring into a cup of steaming tea.

"Hi," he said gently, cutting into her thoughts.

She looked up to see him tucking his shirt into his pants. They stared at each other for an awkward moment and then both of them spoke at once.

"Would you like some—"

"I guess I'd better—"

"You first," Sean conceded, with a half-smile.

"Would you like some tea? It's freshly steeped."

For a few more moments with you, of course.
"Yeah, that sounds good."

For several moments they faced each other across the round wooden table. The only sounds were the light sipping noises as they drank their tea.

At some point she had to come to grips with her life, she thought, as she inconspicuously watched Sean's profile. Yet there was that deep, dark corner of her heart that told her that happiness was not to be hers. She must pay for what happened to Tony.

Sean looked up from his cup and saw the tortured look that hung in her eyes. A sharp pull ripped through his gut. He stretched his hand across the table and stroked her smooth knuckles.

Khendra's lips twisted into a semblance of a smile before she spoke. "I guess you think you've really hooked up with a nut case," she said in a low voice.

"I don't know what to think at the moment. You haven't told me anything."

She shook her head, sighed deeply and rose from the table. Sean got up from his seat and followed her. Walking toward the terrace, she slowly, painfully began to speak. The need to exorcise her heart was more powerful than she realized.

"It had been raining all day. We'd gone to the company party—Tony and I." She hesitated.

Sean stood next to her on the terrace, his muscled arms braced against the white railing, and waited for her to continue.

"He'd been drinking and we'd gotten into a terrible argument about my work, right in the middle of the

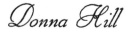

room. He always felt so threatened by my success, no matter how much I reassured him." She hesitated again, and stared out at the cloudless sky.

"There were a lot of important attorneys, judges and politicians there and Tony began making a scene. I knew he'd had too much to drink." Her voice broke, as hot tears crept down her cheeks.

"Ssh, you don't have to tell me anymore. It's okay," Sean soothed. He put a comforting arm around her shoulder and pulled her next to him.

"But I shouldn't have let him go," she sobbed. "If I had only...oh, God!" Silent sobs racked her body as she clung to Sean.

"It wasn't your fault, Khen. You can't go on blaming yourself."

She continued on as though she didn't hear him, compelled by something deep within her that needed release. "They said...he...just walked right out...in front of the truck."

Sean cringed inwardly at the vision and pulled her tighter. "You couldn't have known," he said softly.

"But he needed me so much and I wasn't there." She turned dark, misty eyes toward him. "I wasn't there! How could I ever think about being happy again? I don't deserve to be cared about." She turned and walked back into the living room.

Sean walked behind her, caught her by her

shoulders and turned her to face him. Pushing her to arm's length, his smoldering eyes riveted her with their force. "Now you listen to me, and listen good! I've waited all my life to find someone like you. And now that I've found you, I'm not going to settle for what you just told me."

"But Sean, you don't—"

"I said *listen.*" Khendra instantly knew he meant business.

"There's no way you could have known what was going to happen. I'm sure if you did you would have stopped him. But I'm here now, and you're here. We have a chance—together. But only if you're willing to let it happen. I am, and I know I can make you happy."

Khendra hung her head. Her heart pounded in her chest. She wanted to leap into his arms, sink into the comfort of his words. Could it be possible that happiness was only a breath away? Did she dare take that chance and risk losing again? She looked up into Sean's eyes and saw the look of sincerity and genuine caring that filled the dark depths. Suddenly she knew she was willing to try.

Slowly she stepped into his arms, her eyes searching his face. Then she placed one, soft tentative kiss upon his lips. Sean seemed to draw in all the air around them as he pulled her into his arms and covered her lips with his own. His hot tongue parted her lips, rediscovering the moist cavern. He stroked her back, her hips, her thighs. Finally his fingers inched their way under her belted kimono to stroke the silken nakedness beneath.

Khendra sighed as the warmth of his touch began to methodically melt the icy doubt that had formed around her heart. She felt herself, once again, giving in to the pleasure of Sean's artful caress. Questions sought to seep into her consciousness, but she shoved them aside, for the moment wanting only to lose herself in his heady kisses.

Finally, it was he who broke the connection. "I think I'd better be going," he said in a throaty voice, "or else you may never get me out of here."

Khendra smiled tenderly, stroking his smooth brown face with a slender finger. "I had a beautiful evening."

Sean put a finger to her lips. "Don't say a word, or you won't get rid of me. I'm warning you."

"All right. But I have to say one thing. I...I just want to thank you... for understanding."

"There's nothing to thank me for, Khen. I care about you." Maybe more than I realized. "If we're going to be in this thing, we're in it together."

He stood in the doorway looking down into her bronze-colored face, and was once again overcome by her exotic beauty. He placed a tender kiss on her cheek. "I'll see you tomorrow."

"I'm looking forward to it." And she realized she really meant it.

He turned to leave.

"Oh, Sean."

He looked over his shoulder.

"Thanks for the flowers. They were beautiful."

For a moment he had a puzzled look on his face. "Is that a hint?"

"Hint? Of course not. You did send me flowers, didn't you?"

"I wish I had. And you thought you didn't have any admirers." He smiled and walked down the hallway.

Khendra's heart pounded in her chest, as she closed the door. If Sean didn't send them, then who did? She didn't want to think about the possibility.

Chapter Ten

For the next few weeks, Khendra floated on cloud nine. All of her hours away from work were spent either thinking of Sean or being with him. So much had happened in such a short span of time. At certain moments she still couldn't believe her own happiness. She had even told him about her initial animosity toward him when he first arrived at the firm. Now, instead of a bone of contention, it was a standing joke between them.

What added to her aura of peace was that Alex Counts was out of town on business. However, he made it perfectly clear, via his personal secretary, that they would talk when he returned. Even though she had immediately disposed of the flowers once she realized they were from him, she still could not rid herself of the sense of foreboding that hovered on the fringes of her happiness. Today he was due to return.

Not knowing what to expect, Khendra was agitated. She paced her office like a caged lioness. As she walked, she nervously twisted a button on her trim-fitting magenta linen suit, and occasionally patted her hair into place.

Taking a halting breath, she paused in front of the large window, looking at the wide expanse of blue sky that canopied the bustling, colorful city. Momentarily, she visualized herself and Sean walking hand in hand, as they often did recently, meandering in and out of the myriad of shops and cafes along the historic walkways.

A soft smile of contentment pulled across her smooth face, lighting her eyes. As much as she was afraid to admit it, she was falling, and falling hard for Sean Michaels. There was no denying the powerful attraction she had for the man. Just thinking of him made the pulse pound in her head, and she felt a slow hot flush spread over her as she relived his drugging kisses and his masterful caresses. *Slow down, girl,* she chided herself, with a silent chuckle, *there's nothing as good as being there!*

Turning away from the window, her smile was immediately replaced by a look of alarm and annoyance. She didn't know how long Alex had been standing there, and it didn't matter. All she felt at that moment was a sense of being stripped bare, almost as if

her thoughts had been invaded by the most cunning of voyeurs.

"Mr. Counts," she said, straining to keep the edge off her voice, "I didn't hear you knock."

A half-smile played on one side of his mouth, stretching his thin lips into what almost looked like a leer. An involuntary shudder ran up Khendra's vertebrae. Quickly regaining her composure, she took a seat behind her desk and clasped her hands together.

"It's good to see you again, Khendra." Alex strolled around the office as he spoke, fingering the ivory and porcelain objects that decorated the room. "How have you been since we last spoke? I assume you received my apology."

Snippets of their last conversation buzzed through her brain, and remembrance of the scent of the roses rolled in her stomach. Clearing her throat, she sat ramrod straight in her chair. "I've been fine, thank you. And as for your gift, it was totally unnecessary." *And unappreciated,* she wanted to add, but didn't. "Was there something specific you wanted to discuss with me? I received your message from Phyllis."

She was almost certain he could hear her heart hammering in her chest, even though her crystal-clear voice held no trace of the nervousness that threatened the facade of her Oscar-winning poise.

"There are quite a few things I want to discuss

with you, as I mentioned." He stopped in front of her desk, placing his palms on the cool, hard surface, and leaned toward her. "That's why I made early dinner reservations. We can talk about your future." His electric blue eyes bore into hers.

The combination of his cologne, mixed with the lingering scent of tobacco, swam through her head. She felt totally vulnerable in her seated position, and smoothly rose to her full height. "I have plans for this evening, Mr. Counts," she said with as much calm and conviction as she could summon.

"They couldn't be as important as your future with MC&P, now could they?"

Her soft brown eyes darkened in disbelief. "What are you saying? If I don't go, my job is in jeopardy?"

Alex let out a derisive chuckle and moved away from her desk, walking across the room. Then in a low, controlled voice, he stated simply, "I would never say anything like that." He turned to face her. "However, there comes a time when we have to make choices concerning our careers—things that will either advance it, or hinder it. The decision, of course, is yours."

Khendra's mind raced in every conceivable direction at once, as frame by frame she saw her years of hard work and dedication deteriorate. She felt trapped, seeing no immediate way out. She would give in, for the moment, until she found out definitively what this man had up his sleeve. If he wanted to play a game of innuendo and deception, she could be just as good at it. She tilted her chin in a subtle gesture of challenge, looking Alex directly in the eyes. "What time should I meet you?"

Much to Khendra's dismay, the day sped by at an unbelievably fast pace. Her morning court session was grueling. She was glad when the judge recessed for lunch, but her feelings of unease heightened. It was only a matter of hours before the day ended and she would have to meet Alex. He had made reservations for six-thirty, and she would somehow have to find an excuse for canceling her dinner date with Sean.

She checked her gold watch. Sean was due to meet her shortly in the courthouse lobby, after trying a case in the adjoining building. Her heart raced as she packed her briefcase. Then, the absurdity of her behavior hit her. She had nothing to hide from Sean. If anything, he might be able to help her. At least if she explained to him what was going on, he might be able to offer some suggestions on how to combat Alex without losing her job and everything that went with it. She had been reluctant to discuss the mounting situation with Alex because she didn't want Sean to get the wrong idea. But she was finally beginning to feel secure enough with him to include him not only in the good, but the troubling spots of her life as well. If they were going to make this thing between them work, she was going to have to stop being so afraid.

Taking a deep breath and feeling somewhat better about her decision, she strolled purposefully out of the courtroom, her heart smiling with every step as she made her way down the corridor to wait for Sean.

Khendra paced the lobby, and briefly criss-crossed the steamy pavement, as she watched the sea of harried faces streaming by. But Sean's face was not among them. Checking her watch one final time, she realized she could wait no longer and returned, reluctantly, to the courtroom. Confusion and disappointment fought for first place in her emotions. Once the court proceedings began again, however, she was able to temporarily put Sean out of her thoughts. But she still could not shake the uneasy feeling inside of her.

⊱⊰

The small, intimate Italian restaurant was dimly lit and soft music played in the background. Alex had already arrived, when Khendra entered the restaurant. She was immediately taken to his table and, as she approached, he rose to greet her.

"What would you like to eat?" he asked, when she had settled herself in her seat.

Khendra was nervous and agitated about being there and also because she hadn't had an opportunity to talk with Sean. Food wasn't on her mind. "Will you order for me?" she asked, as she watched the waiter fill the crystal goblets with water.

Khendra quietly surveyed the tastefully-decorated room, as Alex scanned the menu. He ordered mussels as an appetizer, the house salad, veal with sage in white wine, and fettuccini with pesto for them both, and a bottle of wine.

"Do you come here often?" she asked, attempting to make conversation when he had returned the menus to the waiter and rested his eyes on her.

"I bring *special* people to dine here from time to time." He took a sip of water from the delicate goblet and looked at Khendra over the rim of the glass. "You're a very beautiful woman, Khendra. But I'm sure you know that."

"That couldn't be the reason you asked me here tonight."

"Let's put business aside for now, shall we? I'd rather you just sit back and relax. Enjoy your meal and we can talk later."

"I'd prefer to get this out of the way." Her tone

was calm but clear.

Alex, sensing Khendra's mood, decided to try another tactic. He could wait. "Why don't you fill me in on the case you're working on."

Khendra still wished he would get to the point, but she leaned back in the soft-cushioned chair and began to relate the details of how she was handling her latest case. She talked until the waiters began serving their meal. She was starting to relax a little, as they began to eat heartily. Maybe she would get through this after all. As Khendra turned her head to ask the waiter standing nearby to refill her glass with water, she saw something that caused her heart to momentarily freeze. She had turned just in time to see Sean exiting the restaurant, his arm casually wrapped around a tiny waist.

Chapter Eleven

For several seconds, Khendra couldn't keep her heart from hammering in her chest. She went through an array of mental explanations for why he would be there with another woman. It was obvious from the intimacy of their contact that he knew the woman very well. She could think of no explanation that would make the feeling of betrayal disappear.

An overwhelming sense of hurt and anger engulfed her at once. Her appetite was gone and she completely lost track of what Alex was saying. It wasn't until he placed his hand on hers that she even remembered he was there.

"Where did you just go?" he asked, breaking into her troubling thoughts.

"I...I'm sorry. I thought I saw someone I knew." She swallowed the lump that had formed in her throat. "But I guess I was mistaken."

Alex briefly looked in the direction that had caught Khendra's attention, an inquisitive look lifting his brow. "I see. Well, I certainly hope it didn't bring back any unpleasant memories. I want this evening to be special." He smiled at her invitingly.

She immediately dismissed his look and his remark. She looked him squarely in the eyes, forcing her emotions beneath the surface. "I was under the impression we were here for a business dinner and nothing more."

"Of course. But I'm sure we'll find other things to discuss as well," he replied in a controlled voice.

Khendra finished what she could eat of her meal and nervously checked her watch. "It's getting late, Mr. Counts, and I have quite a few things to do this evening, so if we could get to the point."

"That's what I admire so much about you, Khendra. You don't mince words. You're direct and assertive. I like a woman who isn't afraid to say what she feels." His eyes roamed over her as he spoke. "That's why I feel so sure that making you a partner would be good for the firm."

"Thank you. But I thought we discussed this already."

Alex had finished eating and took a sip of wine before he spoke. "You're a bright girl, Khendra. I'm sure you realize that nothing comes easy. You would be the first female partner the company has ever had. And it would be based on my endorsement."

"Are you trying to tell me I would never be offered this opportunity based on my own merit?" Her voice rose in astonishment.

"I would never say such a thing," he said, smiling cautiously. "However, without inside support, it would be extremely difficult."

"Why are you telling me this?" she asked, trying to keep the exasperation out of her voice.

"Because I like you. I like you very much. And I think that together we can do wonderful things."

"I'm sure you're referring to the job."

"Why of course, my dear. What else would I be referring to?"

Khendra knew that her experience with men was limited, but she knew a double entendre when she heard one. "As long as we understand each other."

"Yes. But as I mentioned before, nothing comes easy. If you want this job, you'll not only have to show the firm you can do it, but me as well."

Khendra was getting tired. "It would be a lot easier on us both, Mr. Counts, if you would just say what you mean."

"I'm sure you're quite aware of what I mean." He gazed directly in her eyes. "I've invited a select group of friends out to my boat next weekend for dinner and dancing. I'm sure you'll attend this time."

She took a deep breath and rapidly explored her options. This was all too much to focus on, especially when thoughts of Sean and the woman kept infiltrating her mind. She would work it out later. Now, she just wanted to get out of there. "What day?" she asked finally.

Khendra dropped her bag on a chair and kicked off her shoes. She was glad she didn't have to concern herself with making excuses to Alex about driving her home, since she had her own car. Anxiously, she walked to her answering machine to check her messages. Anxiety gave way to disappointment when the only message was from Charisse, wanting to know when they could get together for lunch.

Plopping down on the sofa, her mind raced back to thoughts of Sean not keeping his appointment with her earlier. Then the troubling scene at the restaurant surged back into focus, and her imagination began to run rampant, conjuring up all sorts of pictures of Sean and the mystery woman.

Stop it! Just stop it! she scolded herself. *He wouldn't do that to me. I just know he wouldn't. There has to be a perfectly reasonable explanation, and I*

know as soon as I talk to him, he'll clear this up.

She held onto that fleeting hope as the evening hours slowly slipped away. The sun was just peeking over the horizon when total exhaustion finally seduced her, enveloping her in the total silence that had kept her company throughout the long night.

Chapter Twelve

Khendra sat behind her desk sifting through the assortment of notes and transcripts she had to review prior to her afternoon court appearance. She tried to push aside the throbbing headache from her lack of sleep. Her headache, combined with the thoughts of yesterday's events, made it impossible to concentrate on anything.

Restless, she exhaled an exasperated sigh and walked to the window. It was nearly noon and she had not heard a word from Sean. He had been out of the office all morning and was not expected back. Yet he hadn't called to say a word about having missed their rendezvous.

As the minutes ticked by, her feelings of insecurity became more intense. Maybe it was a mistake to get involved so quickly, she thought, her misery deepening. What did she actually know about him other than he took her breath away whenever she looked into his smoldering black eyes. But how many other women did he have the same effect on? She had been a fool from the beginning with him. She should have followed her instincts.

But he had awakened another side of her that she couldn't deny, a force more powerful than any emotion she had ever experienced. Her thoughts of what he had aroused in her led her to toss her doubts aside. She would let her heart be her guide. Whatever happened, they would work it out, she decided with finality. She had to believe that.

Standing over the kitchen stove, Khendra prepared a light meal of broiled red snapper and a tossed salad. After a long, tedious day in court, she wasn't in the mood for anything too heavy. She placed the plate of food on a tray, along with an ice-cold glass of cranberry juice, and headed for her bedroom.

A cool evening breeze caressed the sheer white curtains, giving the room a tranquil atmosphere. Khendra slipped out of her shoes, sat on the bed with her legs folded, and placed the tray on her lap. She turned on the television and leaned back against the overstuffed pillows, ready to catch the evening news and enjoy her meal. She had just put a forkful of salad into her mouth when the doorbell rang. A brief frown knitted her brow. Now who could that be? She placed the tray aside and padded to the door.

When she glanced through the peephole, her breathing stopped short, and her stomach did an Olympic somersault. But then she caught herself and nonchalantly opened the door, leaning against the frame with a look of total indifference.

"I'm sorry," he said softly.

Her heart almost melted, but she turned the ice back on. "Oh, are you? About what, exactly?"

A devilish grin lit his face and the glacier that had formed. around her heart began to melt. "Are you going to let me in and blast me out, or let me have it out here in the hallway for all the neighbors to hear so I can be totally humiliated?"

"Get in here," she said, fighting to keep a straight face as she grabbed him by the collar of his shirt.

As she gently tugged him through the open door, his eager mouth swept down onto hers, leaving her weak and wanting as the kiss quickly fanned the fires that were barely held in abeyance. He pulled her to him, his own need for her blinding him to the impropriety of their situation. As his desire bloomed hard and swift, he molded her supple curves against him as he stroked her with sure fingers. She clung to him, wanting to rekindle the intimacy she felt she might lose, the intensity of her own need leaving her breathless and trembling in his embrace.

Yet, even as the heated contact between them charged the very air they breathed, a tiny corner of reality clung to the edges of her consciousness. She couldn't let him cloud her thinking with his intoxicating kisses and tantalizing touch. She had to maintain some control, she thought dizzily, as his hot fingers slid underneath her blouse and gently caressed her breasts that grew rigid with his touch. But all thought of control was quickly extinguished when his hungry mouth captured the bud his fingers had released.

Her soft cry of surrender was tenderly swallowed up in his kiss, as his sugar-sweet tongue plunged into her mouth, sending a jolt of electricity coursing through her body. All doubts, and sanity flew out the window, when he skillfully shut the door with the tap of his foot and swept her up into his arms in a single motion, his lips never leaving hers.

He lowered her to the carpeted living room floor and lay on his side next to her, his desire radiating out of his coal black eyes. His mouth descended on hers again, while his fingers opened the button of her skirt and slid it down over her hips. With the agility of a black cat, he eased on top of her, threading a muscled thigh between her yielding ones.

Once again she felt herself slipping under his magical spell, and she knew deep within that she couldn't let it happen. If she allowed him to master not only her body, but her mind, she would be lost forever, and she couldn't let that happen again.

"No, Sean!" she cried, pushing him off other with all of her strength. Quickly she sat up and fixed her clothes, avoiding his stunned gaze.

"What's wrong?" He tried to touch her and she pulled away.

"We need to talk, Sean," she answered quietly.

He stood up and walked over to the sofa, then turned to face her. "All right, talk."

"Isn't there something you want to tell me?"

"About what, Khen," he said, an edge of annoyance tingeing his voice.

"About yesterday for starters." She stared at him hard, her warm brown eyes now cold with doubt and frustration.

Sean took a deep breath, jammed his hands into his pockets and walked out onto the terrace. Bracing his palms against the railing, he contemplated how he could get around what he knew had to be said. It would change everything. Khendra was still so fragile emotionally. He was afraid to risk having her not understand. There had to be another way. At least until he

was sure she felt more secure with him.

He turned to her and inwardly cringed at the cold look of disdain that filled the eyes that had just so recently held nothing but warmth for him.

"Listen, I'm sorry about yesterday, Khen," he whispered sheepishly, reluctant to look her in the eye.

"Sorry! Is that all you have to say?" she sputtered, unable to believe her ears.

"I know I should have called you, but things got so busy and before I knew it, the day had flown by. I knew you would be gone for the day and angry," he rambled on, "so I just figured I'd get some sleep, let you cool off and then I'd try to explain." He looked at her with his easy, award-winning grin, and took a cautious step forward.

"Don't even think about it, Sean!" she ground out between clenched teeth, her hands planted firmly on her hips. The slap of her words stopped him dead in his tracks.

He knew instantly, by her no-nonsense stance and the chill of her words, that she wasn't about to settle for any crap from him. He had to think fast.

"All right," he said in a defeated tone. "I was wrong. There was no reason not to call. I guess old habits die hard. And you deserve better than that."

"What kind of wishy-washy explanation is that? Is that supposed to make everything all right? You've

got to be kidding. Where were you last night, Sean?"
she asked, her question more of an accusation.

A tightness gripped him in the gut, and for a split
second his first thought was to jump on the defensive
and walk out. But he knew that tactic would never work
with Khendra. She was just as stubborn as he was.
She'd never come running after him, feeling that she
owed him the apology, like all the other women. He
would have to tell her something, and fast.

"I told you. I went home...and went to bed."

"Alone, of course."

"What are you—"

She held up her hand to halt any further conversation. "Don't insult me with your lies, Sean. I saw you
last night." A cold knot of fear twisted in his stomach.
"The least you could do is have the decency to tell me
the truth!" She turned on her heel and stormed off into
the kitchen, burning tears of anger brimming in her
eyes.

She felt him come up behind her and her insides
tightened. She wouldn't let him sweet talk her. *Not this
time*, she reaffirmed silently. She crossed her arms
akimbo, her back rigid with determination.

He gently placed his hands on her stiff shoulders
and felt the muscles tighten under his fingertips. *I'm not
going to lose you, Khen. Not now. Not over this.* He
hung his head and sighed deeply, knowing there was no

point in keeping secrets from her any longer, not if he wanted the relationship to work. And he knew deep in his soul that he wanted her more than any other woman he had ever known. "I guess it's about time I told you everything," he said slowly. He took a deep breath, and turned her around to face him. "The woman you saw me with...was my wife."

Chapter Thirteen

She felt her whole body become infused with a kind of pain she had never experienced. Her breathing seemed to halt somewhere between her chest and her throat. The impact of his words was like a vise that had gripped her heart and had begun to slowly and painfully pull it to shreds. She looked at him through eyes that didn't quite see, and for one hysterical moment, she didn't know him any longer.

"Khendra! Khen! Listen to me," he pleaded, seeing her drifting away from him. "It's not what you think. I said *was*." He shook her. "Did you hear me, I said *was*!"

A frown of confusion masked her face. "What are you saying?" she asked weakly, a glimmer of hope lighting her eyes. The urge to knock him out for scaring her half to death released the grip that had wrested her heart.

"We've been divorced for about a year now. Last night was the first time I've seen her in nearly six months." A wave of relief flooded through him once the words were finally out. Now, he just had to assure her that there was nothing going on between he and Carol, and never could again.

"Let's sit down. I think we have some talking to do." He put his arm around her shoulder and felt her relax against him. He briefly shut his eyes, trying to find the words to explain.

≈≈

"...her drug habit nearly destroyed her and me," he sighed, the memories rushing back in waves. "Then her last suicide attempt was the final straw. The newspapers ate it up and me with it. It nearly ruined my legal career."

She reached out a hand to touch his face, as if to wipe away the reawakened pain. "You don't have to talk about it anymore," she said softly. "I know it had to be hard on you."

"But it's over now," he said with urgency. "You have to believe that. Carol is weak. She always has been. I guess that was part of the attraction." He gave a humorless chuckle. "I thought I could be her strength. But she had other ideas."

"Why is she here? What does she want after all this time?"

He briefly looked away from her probing eyes. Do I dare tell you that she has an apartment and plans to stay? He couldn't tell her that—not yet. There'd be plenty of time later. "She says she was in town for a few days and she just wanted to see me. I said o.k."

The next question burned in her throat, but she had to know. "How did you feel...when you saw her again?" Her heart skittered in her chest.

He looked at her, then looked away, his eyes sweeping the room as though searching for the answer. Then his eyes rested on her face, steady and clear. "I...still care about her, Khen. But I'm not in love with her." He shook his head as he spoke. "We went through a lot together. She says she's clean now, but it doesn't matter. I don't believe in going back. She knows that.' He took her hand in his and gently squeezed it.

The flickers of a smile tugged at her lips, as a sense of relief slowly crept through her veins. "You could have told me, Sean," she said without rancor. "I would have understood. I spent too many years with secrets and misunderstandings. I don't want that to be the pattern of our relationship too."

"You mean Tony," he said softly.

She nodded her head. "I never really knew what he was thinking, or what he was thinking about me."

She took a deep breath. "When I did find out, it was too late to change anything. We let too many outside forces and misconceptions come between us. I never had the chance to—" Her voice broke.

"Ssh, it's o.k. That won't happen to us. I swear to you it won't," he said, praying that his words would remain true. He pulled her from her seat on the sofa and onto his lap, cradling her head against his broad chest. "I swear it won't," he whispered against her mouth.

She gave herself up to the pleasure of his lips, letting his persuasive fingers, once again, unleash the well of desire that lay just beneath the surface. It was going to be difficult, she realized, as her fingers traveled over his chest. She was going to have to learn to trust again, to open her heart and love again, and Sean was the man she wanted to experience those things with. But most of all, she had to let him know he could trust her as well, with all of his heart.

She let him know with her touch, so gentle, yet firm that she felt a shiver run through him. A low moan slipped through his lips as she felt his arousal surge through him. She moved against him, impelled by her own passion, and gasped when his rock hard body moved over hers.

She looked up into his eyes, trying to convey all that burned inside of her heart, inside her soul. And in a moment of frightening clarity, she realized the only words that came close to expressing what she felt. She had thought she would never utter them again. She tenderly whispered, as her heart pounded against her chest, "I...love you, Sean."

A light of pure joy glistened in his ebony eyes, and a euphoric elation danced within his soul. He crushed her against him, wanting to absorb her into his very being. His hungry lips seared hers, his tongue delving into the warmth that had become so delightfully familiar. Never before had those simple words meant so much, and he promised himself, at that moment, he would never make her regret them.

Slowly, and with infinite care, he slid her blouse off her shoulders, then eased aside the pink lace bra. He felt her quake beneath him as he stroked her, taunting her with fiery kisses along the cord of her neckline down to her waiting breasts. His hot lips caressed her with scintillating possessiveness.

She instinctively curled into the hard contours of his body, lifting her hips to ease off her skirt and the sheer, pink panties beneath. His hands lightly traced a path over her body, igniting every inch he touched, creating a burning course of unstoppable desire. He grasped her hand, urging her to explore, wanting to again experience the explosive sensations she caused with her touch. His world rocked with sweet agony as her satiny-soft hand enveloped him and the floodtide

throbbed between her gentle fingers.

She felt powerful and completely uninhibited as she boldly guided him within her honey-drenched walls. Sean willingly descended into the volcanic heat that called out to him, plunging into the rippling valley, delighting in the sublime pleasure, while Khendra's long sinewy legs entwined his waist, her breathing coming in long, shuddering moans with his every stroke.

The exquisiteness of their union stirred him deep within his soul. And as he gathered her into his arms, locking them in body and spirit, he quietly whispered in her ear, "And I love you, too, Khen."

Chapter Fourteen

As she prepared breakfast the next morning, Khendra realized she had never felt so alive. The very air she breathed seemed to take on a new vitality. She moved through the sunny kitchen as though walking on air, her heart light, her soul uplifted. And all because of the man whose voice was now crooning a soothing tune over the sound of the gushing shower.

The aroma of scrambled eggs, French toast drenched in maple syrup, and sizzling bacon wafted through the kitchen. Khendra hummed a tune of her own as she set the table, adorning its center with a scented candle in a copper holder.

As she worked, visions of the previous night bloomed hot and full, sending jet waves of wanting running through her veins. She thought too, with a sense of serenity, how comfortable she felt talking to Sean. His easy manner, and the sincerity in his soul-stirring eyes enabled her to open up to him. She had finally told him about Alex and his subtle threats, and her determination to win the partnership based on merit. Sean was extremely supportive, and had even offered her some advice on how to handle Alex. "Don't back down," he'd warned. "If you do, you'll never get out from under his thumb." She had every intention of taking that advice. If she didn't get the partnership, it certainly wouldn't be because she hadn't worked hard. If she maintained her standards, she could always hold her head high.

She was so engrossed in her own new-found happiness, she didn't hear Sean sneak up behind her, and she squealed when his cool hands slid under her pale blue satin kimono and caressed the bare skin beneath.

"Sean Michaels!" she screeched in feigned offense, spinning into his waiting arms. "How do you expect a person to get anything done if your hands are always in the way?"

"Then find a place for them," he said in a husky voice, sliding the pads of his thumbs over the rising tips of her breasts.

"I'd be more than happy to," she said, her voice shaky against his moist lips as she struggled to suppress the tingling sensations he had caused to erupt, "but first we eat."

His eyes roamed seductively over her curves, which were barely hidden beneath the sexy sheath. "I know what I want on my menu," he teased.

"Don't even say it," she giggled, bathing in the heat of his gaze. "We have a long day ahead of us, so we've got to eat something. She gave him a hard kiss and backed away, her eyes filled with warmth.

"All right, I give up," he said, reluctantly releasing her and throwing a long leg over his chair as he sat down at the table. "Everything smells great!" he enthused, eyeing the feast. Almost before she could sit down good, Sean had devoured five slices of French toast, two helpings of eggs and bacon, a tall glass of milk, and sat looking at her as though he was still hungry. A flash of amusement danced in his dark eyes as he looked at the astonished look on Khendra's face.

"For someone who acted like he didn't want food for breakfast—"

"Your womanly pride isn't bruised, is it?" he teased, looking at her over the rim of his second glass of milk.

"Not hardly," she countered with a cool confidence.

"Hmm, 'cause good lovin' always gives me a ravishing appetite." His eyes burned a path across her face.

"Is that right?" she asked in a throaty whisper,

rising slowly from her seat and slipping out of her kimono as she stood. She felt the hot flush of desire surge within her as Sean's eyes instantly lit with desire. Smooth as a panther, he rounded the table and pulled her into his arms, his mouth crashing down on hers, hard and demanding, his hands stroking her curves.

"Looks like we're going to be here a while," he said in a raspy voice.

"That's just what I was thinking—"

≈∂©≈

Khendra's Volvo sped across the freeway, while Sean's ever-moving fingers gently caressed the back of her neck as she drove. As the landscape unfolded before him, the darker realities of his dilemma crept in, distorting the scenic beauty.

Carol was going to be a problem. Even though she swore, before he left New York, that she would leave him alone, he felt sure trouble was on the horizon. He sent her money every month, but it never seemed to be enough. That was one of the reasons he had chosen to come to Atlanta. MC&P had offered him more money and prestige than the firm he was with, and the added income had certainly made life without Carol financially bearable. She was always hounding him for more money, and now she was here in the flesh.

A shudder of foreboding raced up his spine, and he tried to force thoughts of Carol out of his mind. He had allowed her to take away so many things that were important to him, he thought, an involuntary scowl distorting his handsome features. He would not let her do it again, especially if she in any way threatened his relationship with Khendra.

"Hey," Khendra called, cutting into his thoughts, "where are you?"

Sean shook his head as though waking from a dream, then turned to her, his troubled spirit lightened by just looking at her. He leaned over and placed a soft kiss on her cheek. "I was just thinking how happy I've been since I met you," he said, his eyes caressing her as he spoke, "and that I'd do anything in my power to keep you in my life."

"Anything?" she asked with a smile.

"Anything."

∂∞

From above, enormous Piedmont Park appeared to be covered with a brilliant human quilt. The wide array of colors and the collage of blankets heightened the festive air. Music blared from radios at every end of the park, competing with the loud talk, muffled whispers and raucous laughter of the growing crowd.

The bandstand stood proudly aloof, flanked by towering black speakers, a headdress of kaleidoscopic lights and a maze of wires. Technicians and engineers hurried across the wooden platform, barking out orders and testing the sound system, oblivious to everything except their efforts to achieve perfection.

A warm evening breeze gently stirred the blooming foliage and threaded seductively through the swarming masses, while the setting sun threw rainbows of orange and gold lights across the cloudless sky.

Khendra snuggled against Sean's broad chest and munched on an apple while they waited for jazz great, Joe Williams, to open the show. "This is one of the biggest musical events in Atlanta," she remarked as she scanned the crowd.

Sean stroked her unbound hair as he leaned on his elbow. "Do you come here every year?"

"I try," she said in a dreamy voice, relaxing under his gentle caress. "I've loved jazz for as long as I can remember." She gave a soft chuckle. "It was the one thing my parents and I had in common."

"Do you keep in touch with them?"

"Pretty much." She shrugged. "It's just that they still refuse to accept what I do...seeing my name in the papers connected with some of the cases I've handled doesn't sit well with them. Things like that. They just can't see how I can make a living from other people's misery." She shook her head sadly. "All I ever wanted was for them to be proud of me."

"I'm sure they are, Khen," he softly assured. "It's probably just hard for them to admit."

"But I've worked so hard." She turned large, sad eyes to him. "That's why this partnership is so important to me. They'd have to see that it was all worth it."

Sean gathered her in his arms and dropped comforting kisses in her fragrant hair, his eyes drifting off in contemplation. What would it be like to have his woman as his superior? The vision vaguely troubled him, but was quickly extinguished when the stage lights glared on and the crowd roared its approval.

"The show should be starting pretty soon," Khendra yelled over the din.

No sooner had she spoken than the emcee ran on stage and began pumping up the crowd for Joe Williams' performance, to be followed by Roy Ayers, and then Grover Washington, Jr., accompanied by song stylist, Phyllis Hyman. The crowd stomped and cheered, while vendors hawked their wares among them, the air filling with the aroma of hot dogs, spicy mustard and butter-drenched popcorn.

Sean repositioned himself, leaning against a huge weeping willow tree, and then braced Khendra between his hard thighs, hugging her to him with powerful arms. Looking over her head toward the stage, his breath suddenly stopped short. Then surprise quickly switched to annoyance, as the figure approached them.

"Sean, are you okay? Your whole body is stiff as a board." Khendra twisted her body to look at him, but before he could respond, a shadow fell over them and Khendra looked up into a smiling face.

"Hi, hon," came the childlike voice, which in no way fit the figure that came with it.

Carol Gordon-Michaels was anything but a child. Although tiny in stature, her fully-formed curves and stunning legs could easily have evoked envy in any woman. "High yella" in complexion, her gray-green eyes and jet black, curly hair were a breathtaking combination. She barely wore any clothes. The little white shorts outfit she had on was merely a token, leaving little to the imagination.

Khendra realized with dismay that Sean's heart was pounding against her back as he looked upon the familiar face. Her imagination went erratically wild. She snapped her head in his direction, but was quickly reassured when his smoldering dark eyes glared at the figure before him.

"I didn't know you were interested in jazz, Carol."

"There's a lot you don't know about me, Sean," she replied in a bell-like voice, totally dismissing

Khendra as her eyes hungrily raked over Sean.

Sean gathered Khendra closer. "Carol, this is Khendra Phillips. Khen, my ex-wife, Carol."

Carol's laughter tinkled in the warm air. "You say that with such distaste, Mickey."

The endearing term sent a shudder of alarm racing through Khendra's veins. She felt Sean's thighs tighten around her waist. She unconsciously stroked his leg, her eyes never leaving the compelling face above them.

"It didn't use to be that way," she cooed, her eyes turning a smoky gray.

"Is there something in particular you want, Carol?" he asked, his voice taking on an icy edge.

"Oooh, aren't we testy these days." She turned her unusual eyes on Khendra and spoke in a conspiratorial tone. "I can tell you how to fix that," she giggled, bending her hand at the wrist. "After that he's a pushover."

Khendra's jaw clenched, and she fumed at the intimate innuendo.

Sean felt Khendra was ready to spring, and he firmly planted his hands around her waist. "I'm sure you're not traveling alone, Carol. Isn't your escort going to miss you."

"Of course, but then it's always worth the wait," she said in a sultry voice. "Now isn't it, Mickey?"

There's that name again, Khendra thought, seeing red.

"Well, see you two around...I'm sure." She turned and sashayed away, leaving her soft scent behind.

Sean felt Khendra slowly relax, even as he let out a relieved breath. Khendra pulled herself out of his hold and twisted herself around to face him. She opened her mouth, just as Sean's hand came up to stop her.

"Don't say it," he said with an audible sigh. "Carol has got to be one of the biggest mistakes I've ever made."

"That wasn't what I was going to say," she snapped, alarming herself at her tone. She took a calming breath. "'It's just that...at first I thought...that you were really turned on by seeing her," she blurted out.

"What!"

"Your heart was hammering so fast, I thought it was going to jump out of your chest," she accused.

"Carol has a knack for bringing out the worst in me, that's all," he said in disgust. "Listen, we came here to enjoy ourselves." He rubbed her back. "Let's not let Carol ruin that."

Khendra sighed deeply and reluctantly agreed to let the troubling subject drop. But even as the band smoothly slid into Joe Williams' first number, the shadow of Carol's presence hung heavy in the evening air.

⋙⋘

"What do you wear to a yacht party, dah-ling?" Sean asked in a slow drawl. He stood in the doorway of the bathroom with a towel wrapped around his narrow waist.

You look thoroughly edible. "I couldn't tell you. This is a first for me too," she replied, wondering briefly how Alex would react when Sean showed up with her.

She slipped into a pair of white rayon pants and gingerly stepped over the pile of law journals Sean had deposited in the center of his living room floor.

"We could just as well forget the whole thing and stay here," he said in a husky voice, as his eyes trailed over her half-dressed form.

"I think not," she replied, snatching the towel from around his waist and giggling merrily as she quickly sidestepped his reach.

Sean was instantly at her heels, wanting nothing more, at that moment, than to make love to her. He was just about to grab the waistband of her slacks when the phone rang.

"Damn! Saved by the bell," he growled. He picked the towel up from the floor and tucked it back around his waist as he strode toward the phone.

"Hello," he barked into the phone, his mischievous eyes locked on Khendra's face. Then the playful look was gone and he slowly lowered his head, his voice muffled.

Khendra only caught snatches of the conversation, but her senses were instantly alert as she pulled on her electric blue blouse and fastened the buttons.

I told you not to...I don't care...listen, I'll call you when I have it." He slammed the phone down in its cradle, a murderous look in his eyes.

"What was that all about?" she asked in what she hoped was a casual tone.

"Nothing," he lied, not wanting to discuss the matter. It would only complicate things, he decided. "Just some unfinished business."

"About the case?"

"Yeah, actually it was," he said quickly, thankful for an explanation he could use. "Reporters...as usual. They've resorted to calling me at home. I've gone so far as to call the papers and tell them that the trial was either postponed or moved to another court, from time to time." He chuckled at his own cleverness. At least that part is true. He'd had to start doing that weeks ago and it had taken off some of the pressure. But now the reporters were getting wise.

"From everything I've seen and heard, things are going well for you."

Sean could see her visibly relax as she spoke and

a sense of relief washed over him.

"Reporters are part of the game," she added sardonically, a nagging twinge of jealousy nipping at her. She quickly shook off the dark emotion. "It should all be over soon."

"You're absolutely right." He stepped over and gave her a quick kiss and held her around her waist. "Now let's put trials and courtrooms out of our heads and try to enjoy this yacht thing." He gave her a crooked smile and she burst out laughing.

"I think you'd better find something more appropriate to wear."

"Well, why don't we step in here and find something together," he urged, taking her by the hand and leading her into his bedroom.

Within moments, wrapped in Khendra's arms, all thoughts of his conversation with Carol were forgotten.

Alex literally glared at Khendra's back, watching her with Sean. It was obvious they were more than just co-workers and the thought infuriated him. He had purposely left his wife at home so that he could have easy access to Khendra. She had made a fool of him, and that was something he would not tolerate. He had offered her the opportunity of a lifetime and she was tossing it back in his face. Did she really think merit had anything to do with it? She was the fool. Now he would make her pay. He tossed his martini down his throat as a plan formulated in his head. He smiled smugly, and moved easily among his guests.

At the first opportunity, he pulled Sean aside and ushered him below deck and into his private room.

Chapter Fifteen

Word spread like wildfire throughout the office. The news was barely on the wire services, but everyone in the office had already heard the news.

The conference room was filled with well-wishers when Sean entered, exhausted but jubilant. It was finally over. He had defended one of the most difficult and precedent-setting cases of his career. He had actually been able to prove that the defendants had not bombed the clinic. The district attorney had even approached him and congratulated him on his victory, mentioning that Sean would be hearing from his office in the future. He was totally overwhelmed, but all he could think about at the moment was getting to Khendra and sharing his success with her.

His dark eyes shot around the room until he spotted her, even as back slaps and handshakes enveloped him. Her quiet smile seemed to instantly

sooth him, and he knew he could get through the next few minutes as long as she was at the end of them.

She mouthed her congratulations over the heads of the other employees, and that was the only thing he could hear. He tried to graciously move in her direction, but Alex cornered him, clamping a sturdy arm around his shoulders.

"Excellent job, Michaels," he boomed. "I knew we did the right thing by hiring you. Things were getting pretty stale around here," he added, deliberately taking a barb at Khendra as she approached them.

She stiffened at the remark, but maintained her outward calm. She walked away to the refreshment table, where she took a glass of sparkling water and made idle conversation with one of the law clerks.

"I'm sure that's not the case," Sean said, quietly.

"It doesn't really matter, I have big plans for you." He ushered him to the corner of the room and they spoke for several minutes in hushed whispers. Finally they shook hands and Alex led Sean to the head of the conference table. He tapped ceremoniously on a glass and the room slowly hushed.

"Ladies and gentlemen, as you are all aware, Mr. Michaels has just won one of the biggest cases this firm has seen in a long time." Loud applause filled the room. Sean looked confidently out at his peers. "And success cannot go unrewarded. Therefore, I am placing Mr.

Michaels in charge of litigation, which will free up more of my time." He patted Sean on the shoulder and Sean shook his hand.

Khendra stood in absolute shock. How could this be possible? She had been a trial attorney since the day she walked in the door, and had won every case she'd ever handled. Yet she had never been offered anything like this. Sean had only been with the firm a few months and he was to be in charge of assigning the caseload. It was totally unbelievable!

As anger and frustration fought to overwhelm her, the real reason for Alex's posturing hit her like a speeding train. He was trying to pit her and Sean against each other! What other reason could there be? But what was more infuriating, Sean was falling neatly in line with Alex's plan. She had to warn him, but that would come later when they were alone. She was certain that once Sean realized what Alex was doing, he would back out of the offer.

Taking a deep breath and forcing herself to stay calm, she managed to get through the balance of the celebration without missing a beat.

≈⊷

"What do you mean you're going to take his offer?" She couldn't believe what she was hearing.

"You're making entirely too much of this, Khen."

"Don't *Khen* me! You can't be so blind that you don't see what he's doing. For God's sake, Sean, wake up!" She slammed the pot in the sink.

"Listen, I know what I'm doing."

"Oh yeah, and just what might that be?" she fumed.

"Once I get the spot, I can get the best cases for you and me." He smiled as if he had uncovered some treasured secret.

"You really don't see it, do you?" She swallowed back the lump that had formed in her throat. Her disappointment in Sean was so acute it was a physical pain. "I think you'd better go, Sean. I really feel like being alone tonight."

He reached out to touch her and she pulled away. "Khendra, don't do this. If what you say is true, then you're falling right into his trap. You're doing exactly what he wants you to do, jump all over me! I'm not the enemy, Khen. Or have you forgotten?" His own anger rose to match hers.

She took a trembling breath, absorbing the truth in his words. She started to speak and her voice wavered. Clearing her throat, she started again. "I...I'm sorry. You're right. I guess I was just so blinded by what happened, I didn't see what was going on beneath the surface."

"We can deal with this thing together," he said, moving toward her. "But not if we're at each other's throat.

She looked up into his eyes and decided she would give it a chance. Sean was right. They were stronger together, not separately. She sighed deeply and nodded her head.

Sean pulled her into his arms and assured her everything was going to work out, and she would certainly get the partnership. But even as he said the words, pangs of doubt rippled through him as Alex's golden promises tripped through his head.

∽∾

Several days later, Alex was sitting in his office going over the firm's financial statements, when his secretary, Stacy, buzzed him on the intercom. He stabbed the flashing button, annoyed at the interruption.

"I thought I told you I didn't want to be disturbed," he barked into the phone.

"But Mr. Counts, the woman on the phone said it was an emergency, and that you'd definitely want to talk to her."

"Well, who the hell is she?"

"She says her name is Coco," Stacy said, thoroughly shaken by her boss' anger.

"What did you say?"

"She says her name is Coco."

"Put her through," he said hurriedly, and picked up the phone.

"Hi, Al."

"Coco, is that really you?"

"Last time I checked," she said, laughing into the phone.

"Are you in town visiting?"

"Something like that, and I'd really like to see you. Daddy said to look you up when I got here, but I've been so busy."

"When can I see you?"

"As soon as you can get here," she said, her voice full of promise.

"What's the address?"

As soon as Alex hung up the phone, he buzzed for his secretary.

"Yes, Mr. Counts?"

"Stacy, when you go out to lunch, I want you to pick up a gift...for my wife. Select something original and put it on my account. Have it wrapped and leave it in my office when you return."

"Yes, Mr. Counts." She clicked off, relieved that his mood had so drastically changed. Although she hated selecting gifts for her boss, she had gotten used to his requests. This would at least give her some extra time during her lunch hour and maybe she'd find something nice for herself in the process.

Alex spun around in his chair and faced the window, a smile of anticipation lighting his stern face. It had been a long time since he had seen Coco and his pulse throbbed with thoughts of an evening with her. If her father ever found out—he shook his head in amusement.

Chapter Sixteen

"So, how are you and lover boy doing these days?"

Charisse quipped as she slid an iron over a yellow print blouse.

"Things between us are great," Khendra replied in a dreamy voice.

Charisse looked at her friend with a sly smile. "They must be. I haven't heard from you in weeks."

Khendra leaned back on the sofa and twisted her lips. "I'm sorry, but you know how things can get. We've been trying to work things out and get on a solid footing."

"I thought you just said things were great," Charisse said, picking up an under current in her friend's response.

Khendra took a deep breath. "You don't miss a trick, do you?"

"Listen, girlfriend, if you didn't have me looking over your shoulder, where would you be? So talk."
She finished the blouse and held it up for inspection.

"Well—"

By the time Khendra had unraveled the series of
events, from Alex's subtle threats, to Sean's ex-wife's
reappearance, to his promotion, Charisse was beginning
to get a very bad feeling about the whole situation.

"...and you went along with his explanation for
taking the promotion, even though you say he knew
what Alex was up to?"

"Of course. Why shouldn't I?" she said, no
longer sure of her own actions under Charisse's steady
gaze.

Charisse shook her head in amazement. "Love
is blind, just like the old saying goes. It really never
ceases to amaze me how naive you can be sometimes,
Khen." Disappointment rippled through her deep voice.
"Maybe I was wrong in telling you to pursue this relationship."

"Why?"

"From everything I've heard about Sean, he
sounds like a man out to win. Now I'm not saying he
doesn't love you like he says, but I get the uncomfortable feeling that if it came down to the wire, he'd
choose power over you."

"How can you say something like that?"

Khendra fumed, her inner misgivings camouflaged in anger.

"Easy. He's a man, isn't he?"

Khendra jumped up from her seat. "I thought you were my friend, and that you'd be happy for me," she lashed out. "And the first time I've been happy in who knows how long, you want to throw a monkey wrench in it. Thanks a lot!" She snatched up her jacket and turned to leave.

"Wait a minute." Charisse rushed behind her and grabbed her shoulder. "I've never steered you wrong, Khen. And we are friends, or else I wouldn't give a damn what you did, and you know that!"

Khendra took a shaky breath and hung her head. "I know," she said softly. "And I'm sorry. It's just that I don't want anything to go wrong. Not this time."

"I know that, hon." Charisse hugged her friend. "But you've got to stay objective and see things for what they are. Don't let good looks and great sex ruin that brilliant mind of yours." She gave her a sly smile, which caused Khendra to laugh out loud.

Khendra sat back down on the sofa and folded her slender hands on her lap. "All right, so what do you suggest?"

Charisse slipped on a pair of body-hugging brown slacks, and zipped them up. "I think the two of you need an open, honest talk. Maybe you should try to get away for a few days. And definitely find out about this ex-wife thang. I don't like that one bit," she drawled.

Khendra slowly nodded her head, her own doubts and misgivings resurfacing with force. There was something Sean wasn't telling her, and she knew it. But she didn't want to discuss it with Charisse, at least not yet. She wasn't in the mood for any more lectures. Sean had been acting very strange lately, and disappeared for hours on end with no real explanation. She had the uneasy feeling that Carol was behind it.

"Maybe going away is a good idea," she said finally. "I'll talk to Sean and see what he says. My caseload has diminished considerably, thanks to Alex, and Sean is swamped. But I guess a weekend would be just as good. I could use a breather before the big meeting in a couple of weeks."

"Is that when the partnership is going to be announced?" Charisse called over her shoulder, as she entered her bedroom.

"Yes. And from all the rumors floating around, I'm pretty confident I'm going to get it."

A slight shiver ran up Charisse's back.

∞≈

No sooner had Sean returned from court and

"Yes, Cynthia?"

"Mr. Michaels, Mr. Counts wants to see you as soon as you get settled."

A slight frown creased his brow. "Did he say what it's about?"

"No. But it sounded important."

"All right. Thanks." He clicked off.

Briefly, he paced the room in consternation, clenching his jaw as he walked. If it was what he thought it was, he would have to play his cards right. Everything was falling into place. The only sticky part was Carol. She was becoming a real problem.

Things had reached a point where he didn't want to answer his phone anymore, or go home. He would have to find a way to put a stop to her harassment, and soon. She was ruining his concentration, and Khendra was beginning to get suspicious. He would have to tell her eventually. But it just never seemed like the right time. He'd have to see Carol and soon, and get her off his back. He wasn't going to let her ruin his career again, or his relationship with Khendra.

Damn you, Carol! Slamming his fist against the wall in frustration, he buttoned his steel-gray jacket and straightened his burgundy silk tie. *One thing at a time,* he thought, focusing on the meeting at hand as he strode toward the door. *Let's just see what you want today,*

Alex.

"Michaels, come in and have a seat," Alex said magnanimously, clapping Sean on the shoulder. "I have a proposition for you that I think you'd be very wise to accept." His mouth spread into a thin-lipped grin.

❧

Whenever she looked at Sean's handsome face, Khendra was instantly reminded of mouth-watering, rich dark chocolate. It always took everything she had to keep from reaching out and touching the skin she knew felt as smooth and creamy as whipped butter.

She turned on her side and curled up next to the warmth of her lover. It hadn't always been this way for her, she thought wistfully, as Sean tossed a casual arm across her naked hip. She had never felt so complete and loved by any man like she was with Sean.

Even her life with Tony could no longer compete with the fulfillment she felt with Sean. She was finally beginning to put Tony's memory and the part of her life that she shared with him in perspective. They had something special, there was no doubt about that. But there was always that underlying resentment that Tony had for her, and the need to belittle her.

Things were different now. Sean was a man who was sure of himself and would not feel intimidated by her success. He realized how important her career and her accomplishments were to her, and he supported her all the way. Their weekend together at Myrtle Beach had proven that. He had been more passionate and loving than ever before, and she no longer had any doubts about his love for her.

They had returned early that morning, and had fallen into bed and made exquisite love, then drifted off to sleep, aware they were due in the office in three hours.

As Khendra awakened, the thought of the morning board meeting entered her mind, and her pulse quickened. She was sure her partnership with the firm would be announced. A quick and disturbing thought crept through her brain. She had tried to talk with Sean about her feelings and expectations over the weekend, but he seemed to be uncomfortable discussing them with her, which was totally out of character for him. For so long now, they had been able to discuss everything. At least most of the time. Sean still had that secret part of him he had yet to reveal to her. But she was sure he would in time.

Shaking off her misgivings, she leaned over on her elbow and placed a warm kiss on his ear. A slow smile crept across his dark face as his sparkling eyes fluttered open.

✍

"Come in, Ms. Phillips, and have a seat," Malcolm McMahon said, as the other board members settled themselves around the conference table. Khendra walked nervously along the side of the table and sat down, as the room grew silent. This was the moment she had waited for. "Ms. Phillips, as you know," he droned on in his flat, nasal monotone, "this firm is very proud of your accomplishments. You have proven yourself to be a remarkable trial attorney with a very bright future." He cleared his throat, and looked nervously around at the other partners. She held her breath for the but, and it came with a vengeance.

"But I'm afraid that at this juncture we are unable to offer you a partnership," he continued. "Perhaps in a few years when you're more—"

Khendra felt her knees quake. "In a few years!" She heard her voice rise two octaves higher than her normal range, but she couldn't help herself. It took all of her control to keep from leaping across the massive conference table and poking him in his beady eyes.

"Am I to understand that you're dissatisfied with my performance? Since I've been here, my cases alone have garnered this company..." she paused and flipped open her portfolio, "over ten and a half million dollars."

"Yes, I agree," interrupted Claude Perry. "But

you see, Ms. Phillips, we here at McMahon, Counts and Perry have a very conservative reputation. Our clients frown on any, shall we say, attention-getting tactics."

She saw the slow smile of triumph spread across Alex's face, as he sat in stone cold silence. She felt the old feelings she had experienced in grammar schoolyard battles creep up from her toes, ease into her stomach, slip up to her throat and slide across her teeth. She placed her hands on her rounded hips, putting her weight on her left foot, her head angled to one side.

"Why don't we just say what we mean, gentlemen? I was a token, to make this lily-white firm a little more reputable in the eyes of a socially-conscious town. However," she continued, her voice taking on the same steely edge she used in the courtroom, "it's not good business sense to make that same token a partner in this turn-of-the-century law firm. And a woman at that! Your pseudo-liberal mentality hasn't allowed you to digest that yet. You've done your bit for equal opportunity."

"Ms. Phillips! I resent the—"

"*You* resent, Mr. McMahon? *You resent*?" Khendra slammed both palms on the table and leaned forward, capturing the entire table with the magnetic pull of her dark brown eyes. "Let me tell you something about resentment, Mr. McMahon. Resentment is seeing all the other kids with new shoes and hoping that your older sister won't tear hers up before it's your turn to wear them. Resentment is having kids shun you throughout school because you're smart. Resentment is thinking you've finally made it through hard work and determination only to have it pulled out from under you by a bunch of spineless old men."

The stunned audience sat in gaped-mouth silence.

Having said all that, she snatched her portfolio off the table and marched toward the door. She took a deep breath, turned and gave one last parting shot. "You've done me a favor, gentlemen," she said with more calm than she felt. "I was beginning to think life was becoming too easy."

She stalked out of the room, never looking back. Standing in front of the elevator, she fought back the burning tears. She would not let them see her cry, she vowed. She wouldn't break. But what in the world was she going to do? She had given this company her best and she wasn't sure if she had anything left to give. The only thing she was certain of was that she could no longer work for the firm. It would totally go against her convictions. She wouldn't be able to look at herself in the mirror, knowing she **sold** out for a seventy-five thousand dollar a year salary.

Stepping into the elevator, she forced her frayed nerves to be still. She had options, she realized, pressing the button for her floor. She would just have to explore them.

Seething with rage and humiliation, she strode down the carpeted corridor toward her office. All she could think about at that moment was rushing into Sean's comforting arms and letting him wash the hurt away.

Turning toward her office, her heart pounded in her chest. Thank goodness. He was at the end of the corridor. She didn't want him to see her so upset, so she slowed her step and tried to compose herself. Just then, two of the other attorneys came from the opposite direction and headed toward Sean, their faces beaming as they stuck their hands out to him.

"Congratulations, Michaels," said the taller of the two. "We just heard you've been given the partnership."

Khendra's breath caught in her throat, and she stood stock still. Her whole body began to tremble. She couldn't believe what she had just heard.

"I don't know how you did it, but put me on your coattails," said the short, stocky tax attorney.

"Thanks," he said, smiling triumphantly, and shrugging his shoulders. "I guess things just worked out."

He turned to enter his office, when he caught a flash of Khendra in her pale pink suit as she ran down the corridor.

Chapter Seventeen

Khendra was devastated. She left work immediately and went home, where she cried endlessly.
Finally she regained her composure enough to call
Charisse. However, the minute she heard Charisse's
voice, she became hysterical again. Charisse was able
to calm her down long enough to insist that she come to
her apartment so they could talk.

Charisse paced the kitchen floor as she waited
for Khendra, thinking about what she should do. What
she had gathered from Khendra's disjointed sentences
was that Sean had been given the partnership, and
apparently he knew he was going to get it all along.
That bastard. If she ever got the chance to—Well, there
was no point in thinking about that now. She had
Khendra to think about.

She ran to the door immediately, when she heard
the loud knock. She opened the door and Khendra fell

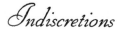

into her arms, sobbing.

"Settle down, hon," Charisse soothed. "Everything's going to be o.k."

"Oh, Cee Cee, I can't believe this is happening to me," Khendra sputtered between choking sobs.

Charisse led her to the sofa and sat her down. She sat beside her, placed her head on her shoulder, and rocked her until she was still. She was alarmed. She had never seen Khen like this before. Even at Tony's funeral, she was shocked and hurt, but nothing like this.

After much coaxing, she convinced Khendra to drink a cup of tea. She also talked her into giving her the keys to her apartment so she could go pick up the things Khendra felt she would need for the next few days. She had no intention of letting Khen go back home and be at the mercy of smooth-talking Sean Michaels.

She finally convinced Khendra to go into her bedroom and lie on the bed. Khendra was exhausted, and within minutes she was asleep. Charisse sat on the edge of the platform bed and stroked her hair. She was so angry she wanted to scream. How dare Sean hurt her friend like that? Of all people, Khendra certainly didn't deserve this. And she blamed herself. If she hadn't pushed her into seeing Sean, none of this would have happened.

She pulled the blue-striped sheet up around

Khendra's shoulders and tiptoed out of the room. She sighed in disgust, as she picked up the keys from the coffee table and headed for the door.

～～

Sean paced the floor of his office, running his hands across his head, pain and anxiety etched in his face. Where was she? It had been three days since he last saw her, and the word was out that she had sent in her resignation, effective immediately.

He had gone to her apartment and knocked so long and hard, he thought the door would fall down. He had called and left messages on her answering machine, but she never called back. He had tried everything he could think of, and he couldn't remember her friend Charisse's last name to save his life. He was sure she would know where Khendra was staying. He hadn't slept in days, and the strain was beginning to show. Maybe this whole thing wasn't worth it. Not at this cost. He should have told her what was going on from the beginning. Damn it! What have I done? he thought.

～～

Khendra sat on the black leather sofa in Charisse's living room, sipping a cup of peppermint tea.

She looked at the scrawled list in front of her, which outlined the things to be attended to before she moved to New York. She had already sublet her apartment, closed her bank accounts and visited her parents. She was having her car transported to New York the following day.

A hard knot of pain formed in her throat when she thought about how her life had roller coastered over the past few months. Things had changed irrevocably, and the one person she thought she could count on was the one who had hurt her the most.

It had been three weeks, and she still could not say his name out loud without tears coming to her eyes. She had gone over it hundreds, thousands of times, and she still could not understand why he had done this to her.

Now there was just such an emptiness inside, as if someone had dug a huge hole in her being. Instead of the fulfillment she had come to know, there was only pain. She felt her heart well up again in the unbelievable grief and sadness that had become a part of her daily life. But what was worse, and the most painful of all, was that she still loved him, and probably always would.

She knew that he had been trying to contact her, but she didn't want to hear anything he had to say. There was no explanation. She struggled with herself

every day to keep from answering the messages he left on her machine. She longed to see him, to talk with him, to touch him. But she could not forgive him.

As tears of regret threatened to fill her eyes, she sniffed them back and checked the last item on her list. *Call Cliff Samuels in New York and let him know the arrival time of my flight.* She had decided that leaving the city she knew and loved was the best thing for her. It would give her a chance to start over without a lot of haunting memories taunting her at every turn. And Cliff's small, but prosperous, firm held the anonymity she needed right now. He had always told her that if she ever wanted to get out of Atlanta, there was a place for her with his firm.

"You about ready?" Charisse called from the bedroom.

"In a minute. I just have to make that call to New York. Then we can leave," she added solemnly.

"I'll start bringing the bags down to the car," Charisse said, entering the room and lighting comforting eyes on her friend.

Khendra smiled weakly, and dialed.

≈◈≈

Alex sat at the outdoor cafe table and slid the long, gift-wrapped box across to his companion. "This is something I thought you might like."   He smiled broadly.

"Well, why don't I open it later," she cooed in a tempting voice.   Her thinly-arched eyebrows lifted in challenge, as she knew she would just toss the gift into the closet with all the other trinkets he had purchased her.

"Sounds perfect," he said, raising his glass in agreement, his loins throbbing with the vision of once again lying in the arms of this woman who was young enough to be his daughter.

Chapter Eighteen

She walked with an easy grace—long smooth strides, head held high. She moved through the pushing crowd with an ethereal aura that belied the inner turmoil boiling beneath her polished surface.

He saw her before she spotted him, and his heart stopped in his chest. She was more beautiful than he had remembered. There was a serene, almost haunting quality about her beauty now that left him overwhelmed. Her glowing auburn hair was much longer than he recalled, falling to her shoulders in tumbling waves. He had an almost uncontrollable desire to rake his fingers through it and he found himself balling his hands into fists to stave off the vision. Her tailored dark blue suit fit her curves deliciously, her full high breasts pushing against the fabric as she walked. Yet there was no doubt she was a professional, her carriage a camouflage to the fire he knew lay within that proud exterior.

As he shouldered his way through the airport crowd and moved closer, a twinge of alarm caught him off guard. Her eyes—those large, enchanting eyes—were vacant, as if hollowed out by a surgeon's scalpel. They had lost their vibrant luster, the full-of-life look that he remembered so well. All he could think of at that moment was gathering her in his arms, and crushing away the hurt that had, so obviously, left its mark. But of course he couldn't do that.

"Khendra! Khendra!" he called instead, his strong, baritone voice cutting through the din of the airport terminal. He waved his long, muscled arm high above the heads of the crowd to get her attention.

She turned at the sound of her name and recognized him instantly. He was almost the same as he was five years ago. But his rugged good looks had intensified. His thick, dark brown hair showed flecks of gray at his temples, which only highlighted his blatant virility. He moved through the crowd with the self-assurance of a man used to getting his way in life. He wore a beard now, which gave his well-chiseled face a dangerously tempting look. His dark brown eyes were clear and direct, as if he could look into one's soul. Cliff Samuels was a man who could almost make you forget, she thought, her pulse suddenly quickening at the realization. She moved slowly in his direction.

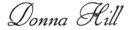

❮❯

"Alex, where are you going at this hour?" Ellen Counts demanded in her reedy voice.

Alex turned toward her slender figure, his eyes ablaze with anger. "I told you before," he growled taking a threatening step toward her, "I pay the bills around here. I buy all those expensive dresses that fill your closet! Don't question me, Ellen. Do you understand?" His voice chilled the air.

Ellen took a shaky step backward, her heart thudding in her chest. She had seen him like this before. Always at the start of a new infidelity he was agitated and short with her, sometimes violent. She hung her head in defeat, knowing that no matter what she said or did, Alex would leave anyway. She took a deep breath, straightened her shoulders and turned away, slowly mounting the spiral staircase to her bedroom.

Alex slammed out of the house, thankful that he didn't have to hit her this time. He hated when he had to do that, but sometimes Ellen enraged him to the point where he couldn't think clearly. He just couldn't stand the whining and nagging, the pleading eyes. He would have left her years ago, but she was the perfect partner for his world. She came from old money and her family was highly regarded in the city of Atlanta. As a young girl, she had been educated in the skills of etiquette, style and grace, and she had been an asset to him over the years.

He gunned the engine of his Cadillac, pulled out of the long driveway that was hidden by a cove of trees, and headed down the winding road that led from his secluded home to the main highway. Soon, he thought, he would be in the arms of a vibrant, sexy young woman. His blood boiled at the prospect.

He had moved her from the apartment she had to a spacious condo in the suburbs. He smiled ruefully. To hell with Khendra Phillips, he thought, taking the wide turn a bit too fast. With Coco in his bed, what did he need with her? He had given her just what she deserved and he was rid of her for good. And Sean Michaels' ego was so big he fell right into the plan.

❧

Sean had memorized every crack and crevice in the ceiling. He had spent so many sleepless nights staring up at it, he had counted them all. He was unable to think, unable to eat. His need to see Khendra was so great, it was a physical pain. A dull throb of unbearable loneliness became his silent companion in the days since she had left. And he knew that without her that void would never be filled.

He never thought any woman would be able to

make him love the way he loved Khendra. A hard knot of despair tightened in his throat when he thought how different things could have been. She was everything he ever wanted, and he was sure that without her he would never be whole again.

The job, the partnership, all the accolades meant absolutely nothing without her in his life. If he had to travel to the end of the earth, he was determined to find her and make her come back to him. She had to understand that what he did was not for personal gain. There was so much that he needed to explain and he had to find her. Somehow.

Pain engulfed him as he rolled out of bed, clad only in black bikini briefs, to stand in front of the window. Brilliant stars filled the midnight blue sky. He stared blankly, wondering what road would lead him to her.

Turning morosely from the window at the sound of the phone, he strode toward the nightstand at the side of his bed to answer it.

"Yes?" he barked into the mouthpiece.

"Hi, sweetie."

His jaw clenched. "What do you want, Carol?"

"I just wanted to give you my address. Maybe you'll stop by and see me.'"

"Now why would I want to do that?"

"We have history, lover. Or did you forget?"

Her voice grew softer. "Besides, I need to see you."

"For what? I've already given you what you asked for."

"Now you know my tastes run high," she cooed. "That only held me for a little while."

"Listen to me, Carol," he boomed, the combination of her call and the stress of needing Khendra coming to a head. "I don't owe you a damned thing! We had an agreement. You blew it by coming here. Now you stay the hell out of my life or—"

"Or what, Mickey? You wouldn't want me showing up at your job, or calling the newspapers to tell them all our little secrets, now would you? I can stand the heat again. I have nothing to lose. What about you?"

His throat constricted as he bit off the words he wanted to spit out at her. All he could think about at that moment was how he'd like to grab her by her slender neck and— The vision sobered him.

"How much?" he asked finally.

≈≈

It was the first time she had really laughed in so long, the sound was almost foreign to her ears. Cliff lightly touched her hand across the restaurant table and grinned back at her.

"It's good to see you smile," he said in a low, intimate voice that threaded its way down to her toes. She briefly lowered her eyes, then looked up at him.

"I guess I haven't had anything to smile about for a long time. It's still kind of hard sometimes."

"Do you want to talk about it?" His eyes searched hers.

She shook her head. She wasn't ready to talk about Sean. The pain and emptiness was still too acute. Cliff had been so good to her since she came to New York. He filled her days with good solid work, and her evenings with dancing, dinner, movies. But—

"I won't press the issue," he said gently, easing into her thoughts. "If you ever want to talk, just remember that I'm here." He took her soft hand, turned it over and placed a tender kiss on her palm, privately wishing it was her full lips instead. "Let's order," he said in a thick voice.

Chapter Nineteen

Sean stepped out into the glaring sunshine in quick, purposeful strides, as he exited the courthouse. The wind blew open his beige overcoat, exposing the charcoal suit beneath. His face was a mask of concentration, his dark profile cutting a stunning cameo against the mass of bodies that surrounded him. To the casual onlooker, he would appear to be a man with the world at his feet—tall, handsome, sexy, secure. But Sean's mind was anxious.

He gripped the rolled newspaper in his hand, tapping it against his hard thighs as he walked. His heart pounded with every step. It had been fate that had drawn him to the arts and entertainment section of the newspaper. And right there in the centerfold was a big spread about the grand opening of an exclusive boutique owned by Charisse Carter.

He had almost stopped breathing when he saw

the name. He was sure that was the name of Khendra's best friend. The article went on to state that it was her second shop and gave the locations of both. His hands visibly shook as he looked at the smiling, confident face staring back at him, and continued to read the detailed account of the one person who knew where he could find Khendra. He had silently cursed the fact that he would be tied up in court all day. The hours had seemed to drag, and he had to struggle to concentrate.

He checked his watch as he slipped behind the wheel of his BMW. The opening had begun hours earlier, but he still had time. He would make her tell where Khendra was. Of that he was sure. He no longer cared what it took to find out.

⊰⊱

The large, mirrored shop was filled to capacity with curious lookers and serious shoppers. A large tray of hor d'oeuvres was set up in one comer, while models displayed the latest fashion creations on the other side of the tastefully-decorated shop.

Charisse was more pleased than she had imagined she could be. Her only regret was that her dearest friend wasn't there to share it with her. The mayor had offered her a position on his legal staff, but Khendra had declined the offer. She believed that the only way she could begin the healing process was to leave Atlanta and Sean behind. Charisse took a deep breath and tried to shake off the sad feeling of loss, forcing herself back into a cheerful state of mind.

She smiled and mingled with her guests, moving confidently through the crowd, when suddenly she looked at the open doorway and her heart almost stood still. The man standing there was easily the most devastatingly handsome man she had ever seen in her life. He stood head and shoulders above the crowd, as he moved into the shop with a self-determination that was magnificent to watch. His ebony features and onyx eyes were a lethal combination. And the thin, silky moustache that outlined his full lips made her hunger for the taste of them. She felt weak in the knees, and a surge of heat rushed to her head as those eyes settled on her and he steadily moved in her direction. Her heart pounded uncontrollably as he approached, her guests totally forgotten as a result of his presence.

"Are you Charisse Carter?" His voice stroked her like an ardent lover and entwined itself in her veins.

She raised her chin and looked him straight in those magnificent eyes. "Yes, I am. And you are—?" She gave him her most alluring smile.

"I'm looking for Khendra. And you're going to tell me where she is."

So this was Sean. Charisse felt her whole body

stiffen with anger and a fear she couldn't pinpoint. She had the unshakeable feeling that this man would do anything to get what he wanted. And he wanted Khendra. It was evident in the dangerous glint that lit his eyes. But Khendra was more important to her than risking her own safety.

"I don't know what you're talkin' about," she drawled through clenched teeth, turning away from him defiantly.

He gripped her arm and spun her around to face him. He bent his head to within inches of her face, the manly scent of him causing her head to spin.

"Where is she?" he ground out. The force of his words ripped through her.

"Take your hands off me," she whispered, looking around nervously, "before I call security."

"Call whoever you want. But I'm not leaving until you tell me where she is."

"What makes you think I can tell you anything?"

He loosened his grip on her arm and the softness that filled his eyes went straight to her heart.

"Because I know that you love her too, and that you want to see her happy. Her happiness is with me, Charisse. I need to tell her that, and you've got to help me." His eyes begged her to understand, but his meaning was clear.

Seconds of painful silence passed.

"Come into my office," she said finally.

Sean breathed a sigh of relief and followed Charisse into her office. "I can't explain everything to you, Charisse," he said when they were seated. "But you've got to trust me. I love Khendra and I want her back in my life. I couldn't tell her what was going on, for her own good. And for the same reasons, I can't tell you."

"You have no idea how you've hurt her, Sean," she said, accusing him with a look from her dark eyes. She saw him stiffen at her words, but gained no satisfaction from hurting him.

"That's why I need to see her, to talk with her. I deserve that much—a chance to make things right between us. Then if she won't listen, I'll stay out of her life forever. I promise you that." His voice implored her, his gaze holding her transfixed.

Her conscience raged a silent battle. She didn't know what was right or wrong any longer when she looked at him. But the one thing she was sure of was that this man loved Khendra with all his heart. And Khendra loved him too.

She took a deep breath before she spoke. "She's in New York. That's all I'm gonna tell you. The rest is up to you."

"Thank you," he sighed, relief flooding his voice. He leaned over and kissed her cheek. "You won't regret this."

"I better not," she said to his retreating back, as
he quickly exited the office. *And heaven help me, I
hope I did the right thing.*

≈≈

"That's right, Phil, I want you to locate a
Khendra Phillips. She's been in New York for about a
month. More than likely she's working for a small legal
firm."

"Have you forgotten how big this city is?" Phil
asked in astonishment.

Sean leaped up from his seat. "I wouldn't give
a damn if it was as big as the continent of Africa!" His
voice thundered through the phone, his eyes blazing.
He felt himself rapidly losing control and he gripped the
phone with all his strength to steady his raging emotions. "I want her found," he said with as much calm as
he could summon.

He and Phil Banks had been buddies since childhood. They had covered each other's backs on more
occasions than Sean could remember. Phil was the kind
of guy you didn't want as your enemy, but he could also
be the best friend anyone could ever have. The only
thing that separated Phil and Sean was how they chose
to attack the system. Phil chose to stay in the streets,

while Sean chose law. Yet at times like this, Sean had more respect and regard for Phil than some high-priced lawyer, or anyone else for that matter, because he knew that Phil wouldn't care what it took to help him.

"Listen, man," Sean said tightly. "I'm sorry." He exhaled deeply and leaned against the wall, briefly shutting his eyes.

"She means a lot to you, doesn't she?" Phil asked in soft-spoken understanding.

"More than a lot. Everything. You've got to find her."

"I will, buddy. I will. I'm on it as we speak. I'll get back to you in a few days. I still have great connections. It should be no problem." *Yeah, right. I might just luck out and find her.*

"Thanks, Phil," he said, his tense shoulders dropping.

"Yeah," he replied, his well-worn tan face carrying a maze of old scars collected during the years he had spent on the streets. *This must be some broad.* "By the way, how's that project coming that you've been working on?"

"I almost have him nailed. Just a few more pieces to the puzzle and I can put the screws to him."

"Great, just hang in there, buddy. Everything's gonna work out. Talk to you in a few days."

❖❖

"So when am I going to see you, Alex?"

Alex leaned back in his leather chair and looked at the clock on the wall. Coco was becoming a nuisance. The initial thrill of being with her again had faded like an old washed-out sheet. She was becoming tiresome. "I really don't know. I have plans," he said evenly.

"Plans? What kind of plans?" Her voice rose to a nagging grate.

"It doesn't concern you, Coco."

"But we had a deal. You take care of me, I take care of you. You promised."

"Well, my dear, promises are made to be broken," he said offhandedly, studying his newly-manicured nails under the desk lamp.

"Then you wouldn't mind if I told good old Ellen about your promises, or better yet—Daddy?"

Alex sat up straight in his chair, tension hardening his spine. "You wouldn't dare!" he hissed.

"Why wouldn't I? I have nothing to lose. You promised to take care of me. And I need something. I need it now!"

Alex ground his teeth, as he tried to think of a way out of the mess he had gotten himself into. He could not let her tell Ellen anything. Ellen had always been aware of his indiscretions, but she never knew the women involved. As much as he sometimes loathed his wife, he never humiliated her that way. What's more, he could not take the risk of this little spoiled brat telling her father. Although her father had retired, his power was far reaching. He could crush Alex with a mere phone call.

"All right. I'll see you later this evening," he agreed.

"Now that's more like it, lover. I'll see you when you get here."

Chapter Twenty

Sean sped across town, heading for Carol's apartment. He had tried to reach her by phone, but there was no answer. If she wasn't home when he arrived, he would just shove the envelope under her door.

As he drove past the run down buildings, the neighborhoods slowly began to change. The streets were no longer littered with trash, but lined with trees. The apartment buildings turned to single-family homes and elaborate condos.

Sean's brow creased into a frown. How can Carol afford to live in this section of the city? He knew she wasn't working and he hadn't given her enough money to afford all this. It didn't make any sense. Unless someone was taking care of her. He gritted his teeth and turned onto the last exit.

Sean pulled up in front of the address Carol had given him, and looked up at the building. He got out of his car, walked to the front door, and dialed the number to her apartment. She answered right away and buzzed him through the glass doors. He ignored the elevators. She lived on the second floor, so he took the stairs two at a time, wanting to get in and out as quickly as possible. All he wanted to do was give Carol the money so he could get home.

He let out a breath and pressed the door chime. Carol opened the door dressed in a pink teddy that revealed her well-curved body. Sean deliberately ignored her tempting pose and brushed past her, stepping into the finely-furnished apartment. He turned to face her.

"Well, this certainly is a pleasant surprise, Mickey. Care for a drink?" she asked in her silvery voice.

"I have no intention of staying, Carol." He tossed the envelope on the coffee table where it landed next to a line of coke. "That's what you wanted," he said, looking at the table in disgust.

He turned glaring black eyes on her. "You're still at it, I see." Contempt dripped from his voice.

Carol shrugged her slender shoulders, ignoring his comment, and locked the door. She looked at him, her gray-green eyes sparkling with desire. "It's been a long time for us, Mickey," she whispered, taking slow, provocative steps in his direction. "It used to be good

Donna Hill

between us. It can be again," she added, stepping right up to him and running one hand down his hip, the other stroking his strong chin with a long coral-lacquered nail.

For an instant, he felt arousal overtake him as she pressed her body against his. She reached up on tip-toe and stroked her tongue along his lips. He felt himself yielding, his lips parting to accept her eager tongue. Then visions of Khendra danced before his eyes. He pushed her forcefully away from him, wiping his mouth with the back of his hand.

Carol staggered back from the force of his shove, banging against a porcelain planter which crashed to the floor, scattering her hidden stash of drugs. Her eyes lit up as if ignited by an inner flame. She lunged at him, screaming obscenities and clawing the side of his face before he had a chance to retreat.

He grabbed her wrists in a vise-like grip, while she kicked and tried to free herself. But he showed no signs of relenting, his own anger quickly becoming a scalding inferno. "I'm warning you, Carol," he said in a deadly whisper.

"Let me go, you bastard," she spat. She tried to bite his hands, and he twisted his palm out of reach, pushing her toward her bedroom. "I'm not gonna let you forget how you treated me, Sean," she yelled. "You can't do this to me!"

She struggled violently against him, ripping the

strap of her teddy and, in the process, exposing a round, firm breast. Momentarily they froze, their breathing coming in rapid, panting rhythms, the raw tension between them mounting. Sean's eyes seared across her breast and briefly riveted on the golden orb. Carol saw him weaken and she slipped the other strap off her shoulder, letting the pink top slither down to her tiny waist. She lifted her chin defiantly, the look of anger in his eyes arousing her.

Sean's lips curled into a twisted smile. "Not this time, Carol. Never again. Got that?" He pushed her onto her bed and stormed toward the door, wiping away the blood that trickled down his cheek with the back of his hand.

Just as he reached the door, a pair of scissors whizzed past his ear and lodged in the wooden door. He whirled around to face her, as she once again lunged at him, long nails aiming for his face. He easily side-stepped her this time, but she lost her balance and went headlong into the closed door, knocking over a brass coat rack as she tripped. She wasn't quick enough to dodge the tumbling rack. Sean made a vain attempt to grab it and missed, and the brass rack landed solidly on her head.

Sean immediately fell to her side, as blood slow-ly oozed from her scalp. His heart pounded. He shook her. She didn't move, but she was still breathing. He looked frantically around the room, then went to the bathroom in search of a cloth to place on the wound. He returned and carried her to the sofa, pressing the cold, wet wash cloth against her head. The bleeding slowed and he applied more pressure until it stopped.

"Why, Carol? Why does it always have to be this way between us?" The question stabbed at his knotted stomach. Then a dark, fleeting thought crept through his brain. He looked at her. His heart pounded. She stirred, moaning softly. He saw that his one chance would quickly end. No, man. Enough is enough.

The figure behind the tinted window of the parked car watched as Sean exited the building and rushed toward his car. His jaw clenched in recognition. When the car sped off, he got out and stormed into the building, his own anger boiling to the surface. He would put an end to this once and for all. But what he found when he put his key in the door and opened it made his job that much easier.

Chapter Twenty-one

Sean sat on the edge of his bed, his large hands hanging over his thighs, head bent. He looked at the phone, reached for it, then stopped midway. Guilt assailed him. He should have made sure everything was fine before he left. But all he could think about at the time was getting out of there as quickly as possible before—

Damn! He slammed a fist down on his night table. He shouldn't have let her get to him like that. He covered his face with his hands, trying to wipe away the vision of her lying so still.

But he couldn't...wouldn't let the incident interfere with him getting to Khendra. Why doesn't Phil call? Rising from the bed, he went to the bathroom and gathered toiletries, which he threw into an overnight bag. Then he grabbed shirts and slacks from the closet. I have to be ready. Satisfied that he had what he needed, he reached for the phone and dialed the airport.

≈≋

Alex's hands gripped the steering wheel of his Cadillac so hard his knuckles began to hurt. Pulling into the driveway of his house, he mentally prepared himself for his wife's accusing looks and silent knowledge. But he would deal with her as he always did.

He checked his watch. They were already an hour late for a benefit dinner engagement. So if she started in on him—well, he would just leave her home.

He chuckled. Now everything was back in order. He took a deep breath and walked into his foyer. "Ellen!" he called up the winding stairway, as he leaned against the heavy cherrywood banister. "I'm home. I hope you remembered to get my suit from the tailor."

≈≋

Sean had spent a fitful night. Over and over, he had seen the coat rack slowly fall toward Carol and he was never able to get to her in time. And then— No! He wouldn't think about it. It was over.

No longer able to stay in bed, he got up and took a long, steamy shower, as if trying to wash away the vision. Draped in a towel, he padded into his bedroom and reached for the phone, just as it rang. He snatched the receiver off the cradle, his anxious voice leaping across the wires. "Yes," he barked tersely.

"It's me, buddy. Looks like lady luck is on your side. I've been on this from the moment we hung up and—"

Sean's pulse pounded in his ears. "Cut the crap, Phil," he growled, his adrenaline pumping.

"Keep your shirt on," Phil retorted, stifling a chuckle at his friend's blatant eagerness. "She's with a guy called Clifford Samuels. He's got an office at—"

Sean's mind raced faster than his shaky fingers could write. He had found her, and he was going to make everything all right. No more lies, no more cover-ups. He would make her understand. The past was finally behind him and he wanted her in his future.

"I owe you one, Phil," Sean said in a shaky voice.

"Forget it, man. This one's on the house. Now all you gotta do is get here."

"I'm on my way."

Phil hung up, and Sean depressed the button to dial. He was interrupted by a fierce pounding on the door, as if someone was trying to break it down. He looked at the bedside clock. It was seven a.m. Now who in the hell can that be?

He pulled a navy blue terry cloth robe from his

closet, shrugged it over his muscular shoulders and went to the door. "Who is it?" he demanded.

"Open up. Police."

Shock waves of dread ripped through him. He flung the door open to see two large men dressed in civilian clothes. The tense, drawn faces that greeted him seemed to reflect in the badges they flashed.

"Yes?" A flicker of apprehension grabbed him in the gut.

"Are you Sean Michaels?" asked a burly detective.

Sean took a defiant stance, legs splayed apart. "I am."

"May we come in?" the detective asked, brushing past him before he had a chance to respond. The other man followed.

Sean, becoming more irked by the minute by this intrusion, stood by the door as the men inspected his apartment. "Just what do you want?"

"I hope you weren't planning on going anywhere, Mr. Michaels,'" the second detective said, looking through Sean's bedroom door at the open suitcase he had placed on a chair. "Because we have a warrant for your arrest."

Sean's head snapped instinctively toward his bedroom, sudden panic rippling through him. "What!" Disbelief and icy fear twisted within him.

"You're under arrest for suspicion of murder."

"Murder?" Sean was incredulous. "Have you lost your mind? I haven't murdered anyone."' Sheer, dark fright gripped him. His heart thudded wildly in his chest.

"I suggest you get dressed, Mr. Michaels, and quickly. You're coming with us," the first detective stated calmly.

"What? I don't understand. Who am I supposed to have murdered?"

"Your ex-wife, Carol Gordon-Michaels. Read him his rights, Murphy," the big detective said to his partner.

Chapter Twenty-two

The teapot whistled shrilly throughout the tiny apartment. Khendra dashed across the carpeted floor in her stocking feet, zipping her camel-colored skirt as she moved to turn off the stove. She was thankful that she didn't have to be in the office until later. Her evening out with Cliff had left her tired.

She smiled. Cliff was a good man. He could probably make her very happy. She sighed, then shook her head. No one could replace Sean. The thought was frightening, but true. And she would not allow anyone else to capture her heart again. She would consume herself with work, and that, she thought weakly, would be enough. She'd been burned once too often.

Straightening her shoulders with resolve, she poured herself a cup of herbal tea and headed for the bedroom to look for a file. As she passed the television in the living room, she flipped it on and set her cup on the coffee table.

"Now, where is that file?" she said out loud, fishing through the folders on her desk. Unsuccessful in her search, she stepped into her brown leather pumps and left the bedroom. She was looking through a stack of papers and folders on her coffee table, when a flash on the television screen caught her attention.

The picture perfect face, devoid of all emotion, with hair that was combed just right, seemed to be talking directly to her.

"...as you can see by all the activity behind me, I'm standing in front of the 90th Precinct in downtown Atlanta—"

The camera panned the expanse of the area, revealing news vans, reporters, police barricades and scores of onlookers.

"...where notable attorney, Sean Michaels, of the law firm McMahon, Counts and Perry, was taken into custody earlier this morning and is being held on suspicion of murder."

The teacup Khendra held in her hand crashed to the floor. She felt an unbearable heat race through her body. The hair on the back of her neck bristled. Her pulse pounded so loudly in her ears she could barely make out what this insane—he must be insane—news reporter was saying.

"It appears that his ex-wife, Carol Gordon-

Michaels, daughter of former New York Supreme Court judge, Bradford Gordon…"

Bradford Gordon! Oh, merciful heavens.

"…was murdered last night in her Atlanta apartment."

Khendra's head began to spin.

"Mr. Michaels, as you may recall, was the attorney who successfully handled the…"

She couldn't breathe.

"…As we obtain further details on this shocking event, we will keep you informed. This is Mark Hampton in Atlanta." He raised his right hand to press his earphone, then raised a finger to get the cameraman's attention.

"This just in," he said, the scent of blood rippling through his voice. "Mr. Michaels has just been charged with the murder of Carol Gordon-Michaels. We tried to reach her father in New York but…"

Khendra's knees buckled beneath her and she crumpled onto the sofa. Her vision blurred with the unreality that danced in front of her eyes.

The voice droned on. She wanted to reach through the screen and grab that lying reporter by the throat and make him take back everything he said.

How could this be happening? She ran her fingers through her hair, her eyes wide with frightened disbelief. It couldn't be true. Could it? She shook her head vehemently. Sean wasn't capable of murder. There had to be some other explanation. But what?

Then a terrifying thought settled on her like a blanket of snow, chilling her. What if it was true? The very idea riveted her to her seat, as a slow steady tremor shook her body. No, it was impossible.

She took a deep breath and tried to calm herself with quiet reason. *There's nothing I can do. Why should I care anyway, after all he's done to me? I'm sure he has excellent representation and he'll get through this with flying colors.* Her eyes roamed the room as she twisted her hands. "There's nothing I can do," she whispered weakly.

In slow motion she turned off the television and mechanically went through the steps of getting ready for work.

≈≋

Charisse strolled down Martin Luther King Drive, her coat collar pulled high around her neck. It was a cold but clear day, and she occasionally stopped to look in shop windows as she walked.

Walking past a home appliance store, she suddenly stopped to stare in open-mouthed astonishment at the image projected on the screen of the television that was playing in the window.

She quickly stepped inside the store so she could hear what the reporter was saying. She stood rooted in front of the set as she listened to details of the story. *Sean—? Murder—?* What in the hell had happened? She couldn't believe it.

Khendra! Oh, sweet heaven. What if she saw this? Maybe it was best that she hadn't told her about meeting Sean. Now this. She had to call her, to brace her. If she didn't know already.

She ran in search of a pay phone, and dialed Khendra's number only to hear hollow ringing on the other end. "Damn!" She slammed the phone back on the hook. She must be at work. If there's any justice in this world, maybe she hasn't seen it.

≈≈

Cliff stepped into Khendra's office and gently closed the door. "What in the devil is wrong with you? You almost look pale."

She briefly looked up, tried a smile that failed miserably, then lowered her eyes and stared sightlessly at the papers on her desk.

Cliff pulled up a chair and took a seat opposite her. "What is it? Maybe I can help," he said, unbuttoning his tweed jacket.

She shook her head.

"How do you know that unless you tell me?"

"Because I know you can't!" she snapped. She jumped up from her seat, turning her back on him.

"Khendra, listen to me. Whatever it is, I'm here." He rose from his chair and moved behind her.

The genuine sincerity in his voice touched the weakened threads of her heart. "Oh, Cliff." She turned into his arms and buried her face against his chest, her pent-up tears flowing onto his cream-colored shirt.

How long had he waited to hold her in his arms, to smell the scent of her hair, to comfort her? He wanted to stroke her, to brush his lips against hers, to feel her tremble beneath him, calling his name. But that would come in time, he thought, gently patting her back and making soothing sounds. She had finally turned to him. This was the beginning.

"Sit down, Khendra," he urged, leading her toward the sofa. He sat next to her, keeping a warm hand on her shoulder. "Now tell me. What is it?"

She looked up at him, her large, luminous eyes filled with glistening tears. "Cliff—" She reached out a hand to place on his, and sighed. Then taking a deep breath, she told him all of the events that had led her to New York.

He felt a tightness in his chest, but his turbulent thoughts remained unreadable as he listened—pain filling his gut with her every word. She loved this man.

There was no debating that. But he had ruined that with deceit. There still could be a chance for he and Khendra if he could make her forget Sean. Make her realize that Sean was not the man for her—that he was.

"...so I had to leave. I couldn't stay. Now this." She looked up at him and took both of his hands in hers. "And you've been so good to me. I want to thank you for that."

He smiled, overcome once again by her startling beauty. He fought down the urge to kiss her lips and tell her how deeply he felt about her. He squeezed her hand instead.

"Why don't I make some calls to Atlanta and see what I can find out. He probably has excellent counsel. But if not, maybe I can recommend someone." He handed her an initialed handkerchief from his pocket to wipe her eyes.

"Thank you for everything," she whispered, a mixture of gratitude and relief flooding her voice.

They rose simultaneously from the sofa, as the phone began to ring.

"I'll get back to you as soon as I hear something. Don't worry."

She nodded her auburn head, then turned to answer the phone. She cleared her throat. "Khendra Phillips," she answered softly. Cliff exited the office, giving her the thumbs up sign.

"You don't know me, but I'm a good friend of Sean's. The name's Phil Banks," the voice came over the phone.

Her heart skipped a beat. Heat flooded her. She sat down. "Yes?"

"He asked me to call you."

Her hand started to shake.

"He needs you to come to Atlanta. He's in trouble."

Her mind ran in a hundred directions at once. "How did you find me? And why does he need me?"

"He asked me to look for you several days ago. I did."

Her heart lifted. "He asked you to find me?" Her voice filled with hope.

"He was on his way to you when the shit hit the fan."

She cringed. "Why?"

"I think you need to talk to Sean about that. Listen, have you seen the news?"

"Yes."

"Then you know what's goin' on. He needs you."

"Why me?" It can't be me.

"Because he says you're, the best."

Khendra finished the telephone conversation and left her office. She tapped lightly on Cliff's office door.

"Come in."

As she entered, he rose from his chair and replaced the phone receiver. "I have some news for you. Not all of it is good." He rounded the desk as she stepped fully into the room. "A colleague of mine has agreed to go down to the precinct where they're holding Sean and find out what he can. But the word is they have witnesses who saw him leave the building where she lived around the time of the murder, as well as others who heard a loud argument. And his firm won't touch this one."

Her shoulders stiffened. But her face remained serene, her eyes clear. "I'm going back to Atlanta."

"What?"

"I have to go. I got a call and—"

Cutting her off in mid-sentence, he went to her side. "What do you hope to accomplish by going back there? There's nothing you can do."

"I can defend him."

"Are you kidding?" Panic gripped him. He knew that if she returned to Atlanta, he'd lose her for good. He had to make her see reason.

"Listen to me," he said with more calm than he felt. "You're too close to this thing. He was your lover, for God's sake. How do you think you could adequately handle—"

"I know him, Cliff," she stated in the same flat monotone. "And I know he couldn't have done what they say he did."'

"Exactly my point. If he didn't do it, then he'll be found not guilty."

"Now that's the most asinine thing I've ever heard you say. Nothing is airtight, Cliff. And there's no one better equipped to handle this than I am." Her eyes blazed with determination.

"You're making a dreadful mistake, Khendra." He was almost pleading. He stepped up to her and held her shoulders. "Let someone else handle this one," he urged. "You're so close to it, you could do more harm than good." He saw her weaken as the truth of his words touched her. He pressed on. "Did you think about that?"

Her shoulders slumped and she slipped into the overstuffed office chair. She looked up at him, her eyes dark with worry and confusion. "Maybe you're right," she sighed heavily.

His heart picked up a beat, and he sat next to her. "I know I'm right. You'll see." He brushed a feather soft kiss across her brow and put his arm around her shoulder, breathing a silent sigh of relief. "You'll see," he said again. "I'll do what I can. I promise you that."

The day seemed to go on endlessly, and still there was no further word from Atlanta. Finally, Khendra packed up her briefcase and readied herself to go home. Every muscle in her body seemed to ache due to the tension that had built up in the preceding hours. She just wanted to get home and soak in a hot tub and try to get the events of the day off her mind.

Cliff had offered to take her to dinner, but she had graciously declined. She knew the reason behind Cliff's generosity and solicitousness and she didn't want to add any more fuel to the fire. Cliff was a great guy, but she could never love him that way. He deserved a woman who could give herself to him unconditionally. She was not that woman.

Walking slowly through the parking lot, she had the eerie feeling that she was being watched. She looked around, but she didn't see anyone. Yet, she couldn't shake the sensation. Quickly, she dug in her purse for her car keys, when a figure came up behind her.

"Ms. Phillips?"

She nearly leaped out of her skin, as goose bumps raced up her arm. She turned and looked into the warmest brown eyes she had ever seen.

"Sorry if I startled you. I just wanted to be sure you were alone."

"What do you want?" The voice sounds curiously familiar.

"I'm Phil. We spoke earlier—about Sean."

Her heartbeat slowed to normal. From the looks of him, she couldn't imagine him and Sean being friends. Phil was of medium height with a stocky build, like a boxer. But he had an aura about him that seemed dangerous and immediately put her on guard. He was definitely a man who had known the streets and violence, and knew how to handle both.

"I've changed my mind, if that's why you're here." She turned to walk away, her heart thudding once again.

He grabbed her shoulder, his powerful fingers boring through her coat. "Listen, lady," he growled, "that guy means more to me than any friend I've ever known and I don't give a damn what I have to do to convince you. But if he says you're his only hope, then you're gonna help him."

"Take your hands off me." She glared at him, her own anxiety giving way to anger. "I've told you, I can't help him. If Sean wants me to find him an attorney, I will. But I can't do it." Her voice began to waver. She cleared her throat. "I just can't." She ran toward her car, hot tears threatening to overflow.

Phil stood back and watched her shaky fingers put the key in the lock. "I hope you can sleep at night," he yelled, his voice echoing throughout the lot. "But I'll

be back every single day until you change your mind. You can bet on it."

Khendra quickly got in the car and sped off, her heart hammering in her chest, his words reverberating in her ears. I'm doing the right thing, she repeated to herself over and over. Aren't I?

Pure exhaustion overcame her as she stepped across the threshold of her apartment. Phil's face flashed before her eyes and she shut them as if to erase the vision. She ran a hand across her forehead and massaged her temples.

The phone rang, and she hurried across the room to answer it. Maybe it's news about Sean.

"Hello?"

"Khen, it's me, Charisse."

A pang of disappointment briefly skittered through her stomach. "Hi, Cee Cee."

"I guess you've heard by now."

"About Sean?"

"Yeah."

Silence.

"Listen, hon—"

Khendra braced herself.

"I didn't want to tell you, but now I think you ought to know—"

Her flight was due to depart in thirty minutes. She had wanted to call Cliff last night, but she knew he would only try to talk her out of it again. But she couldn't just leave without letting him know. She went in search of a phone, and prayed he would understand.

Chapter Twenty-three

The cab sped away from the airport and merged with the rush hour traffic. Khendra leaned back in the seat and quickly pulled out her hastily scrawled notes.

Cliff had been able to furnish her with bits and pieces of information, but so much was still missing. She wouldn't know anything for sure until she spoke with Sean.

Sean. Just the thought of him made her shiver. She thought she would never see him again, and certainly not like this. She stared sightlessly out of the window. What would it be like seeing him again? How would she feel—react? There was so much that was still unsettled between them, and this trial would probably only distance them more.

She would have to remain totally aloof, completely professional. There was no way she could allow her personal feelings to hamper her ability to defend him. *But how can I ever be detached when it comes to him?*

Maybe Cliff was right. Suppose she'd made a mistake by coming? A man's life depended on her. She shut her eyes. She was the best. She'd handled dozens of tough cases, and she'd handle this one to the best of her ability. No matter what he might have done to her, he didn't deserve less than the optimum defense.

Her heart throbbed when she imagined seeing his face, and she quickly rechecked her notes to block the vision.

The 90th precinct was bustling with activity. Officers ushered in their perpetrators, while a weathered sergeant barked orders and police administrative assistants dispatched teams. It was several minutes before Sergeant Bailey was able to acknowledge her presence.

"Can I help you, Miss?" He looked at her with a look of curiosity and disdain.

"I'm Khendra Phillips, the attorney for Sean Michaels," she took a quick look at his name plate, "Sergeant Bailey, and I'd like to see my client immediately."

So this was that hot-shot attorney he had heard so much about, he thought. It always left a bad taste in his mouth when the haves thought that money could get them off the hook. He was sure Sean Michaels was as guilty as they come. And all the money in the world, or pretty lawyers, wouldn't change that. He'd be more than happy to see that he got just what he deserved. He leaned his beefy arms across the worn wooden desk and looked down at her with watery blue eyes.

"Got any I.D.?"

She reached into her wallet and produced her identification, which he perused for an annoyingly long time. He finally looked up, pursed his lips and passed the wallet back to her.

"Everything looks in order."

Khendra bit back a retort, determined not to be irked by this obtuse man. "May I see my client now?" she asked sweetly.

"Hey, Parker," he boomed across the chaotic room, "take this here lady back to the room, and bring Michaels out."

A rather thin officer hurried up to her side and escorted her to the visiting room.

≈◇≈

Khendra paced. She waited for what seemed an infinity, holding in all the turbulent emotions that pulsed in her veins. She could not allow herself to succumb to her feelings. This was a job. No matter what had happened between them. If she permitted her feelings to get in the way, they would be defeated before they began. She'd get his statement and that would be all. That will be all, she prayed silently.

She had her back turned when he entered the room, and nothing could have prepared her for seeing him again.

"Khendra." His voice was a bare whisper of relief that fled up her spine and lodged in her heart.

She turned, their eyes met, and suddenly nothing else mattered. The room seemed to bloom with life, the dreary gray walls vibrated with color, and her heart stood still. She fought down the compelling urge to run into his arms, to wipe away the fear and uncertainty that loomed behind those eyes of midnight. But she wouldn't—didn't dare.

"Hello, Mr. Michaels. Have a seat and let's begin."

She couldn't look at him.

How could she be so emotionless? Couldn't she see how badly he regretted all that had happened, how much he was hurting? All he needed right now was to see her smile, to somehow know that things would be all right between them—that she still loved him. Yet, he had to admire her no-nonsense attitude and professionalism, even in the light of all that had transpired between them.

He took a seat diagonally across from her, but he couldn't keep his eyes from wandering to her face. "Khen, I—"

"Let's get the ground rules on the table. I came because I believe I'm capable of defending you. And that's the only reason." Her heart clenched in her chest at the look of pure anguish that filled his eyes. She swallowed the knot that had formed in her throat. "Now I want you to tell me, in your own words, exactly what happened that night."

Sean looked away, an invisible shroud descending over his eyes, locking his heart. He began his story.

Was she really prepared to hear why he had been with his ex-wife? She had seen the pictures of the crime scene and Carol was practically nude. Did he make love with her? Did he hold her, did he— *Stop it! Just stop it,* she warned herself, trying to concentrate on what Sean was saying. Speculating wasn't going to get her anywhere. She was an attorney. An attorney for a man who had been charged with murder. And her only concern was to build a case and get him acquitted.

His pulsing voice filtered through her thoughts. "...everything just happened so fast. She came at me with scissors...she fell...the coat rack hit her on the head I panicked...she wouldn't move..."

His story was scattered and somewhat erratic,

but she was able to piece everything together. And what she gathered from it all was he did not do it. Never once did he mention the scarf she was strangled with. Yet, who could it have been? Obviously someone else visited Carol's apartment that night. But who?

"Sean." It was the first time she had said his name aloud, and a tremor of remembrance ran up her spine. "Did you see a scarf, a silk scarf that night?"

He looked at her as if she'd asked him if he was from Saturn. "What are you talking about? What scarf? And what does it have to do with Carol?"

"She was strangled, Sean." She looked him fully in the eye, waiting for his reaction.

"What? But I thought...they never said...Oh God, Khendra, I didn't do it. You've got to believe me. I didn't do it. She was alive when I left." His voice was an agonized plea. "You do believe me, don't you? Tell me you believe me." His eyes burned into hers, filled with a tormented waiting.

"I believe you," she said with more emotion than she intended. She quickly recovered. Looking away, she added, "Now what we have to do is find out who did." As much as she hated to, she plowed forward. "I want you to tell me everything about your relationship with Carol, from the time you met, and anything else you think might help."

She rapidly took notes, mindful to keep her feel-

ings in check as Sean laid out the story of their stormy marriage, the ensuing scandal surrounding their divorce, including what Carol had held over his head.

"She had...pictures," he said with obvious hesitation. "Potentially incriminating pictures."

Khendra's head snapped up from her notes, her pulse hammering in her ears.

"Tell me."

"I was at one time involved in uncovering some evidence for a client who was involved in a drug bust."

"Go on."

"I didn't want any more police involvement. They had really screwed things up. The D.A. was going for the maximum conviction. But I was sure my client had been set up. So I decided to go after the dealers myself. She had me followed. And she has pictures of me, clear pictures, of me making a transaction with a known dealer."

She briefly shut her eyes and released a breath she hadn't realized she was holding. "Where are these pictures now?"

"I don't know."

"Does anyone else know about this?"

"Just you."

"Why would she do something like that?"

"The dealer, I found out later, was her lover."

"And you've been paying her to keep quiet ever

since." Her question was more of a statement.

He nodded.

"Why didn't you go to the police?"

"Are you kidding? Who would have believed me? Then when the divorce hit the papers and her drug addiction was publicized, she swore she would tell the Bar Association that I helped to supply her, if I didn't continue to maintain her in a comfortable style of living. And she had the pictures. I could have been disbarred. It wasn't worth the risk."

Khendra dropped her head. The enormity of the deceit and betrayal rendered her momentarily speechless. "Did you at least win the case?" she asked finally, trying to lighten the dark mood that had enveloped them.

He chuckled derisively. "On a technicality."

She took a deep breath. "Your arraignment is set for ten o'clock tomorrow morning. I know the D.A. is going to ask for the maximum bail. Can you handle it?"

"I think I can."

"Good." She closed her notebook, slipped it into her briefcase and rose from the hard wooden chair. "Then I'll see you in the morning. Do you have a suit?"

"I have an extra set of keys over the ledge of my door. Would you pick one out for me?"

His eyes were so tender, his voice so penetrating. She didn't want to go back to his apartment, back to memories of dreams now dead.

"I'll bring it at nine." She brushed past him and signaled for the guard.

He held her arm. Fire raced through her body and she felt her knees weaken.

"I have so much to tell you—to explain." His voice reached that secret place in her heart and she almost forgot where they were and why.

She looked him squarely in the eye. "Does it have anything to do with your defense?"

Anguished silence.

"Then I don't think we have anything else to discuss."

She stepped through the door, her heart hammering madly.

Judge Abramson silently reviewed the file in front of him. Slowly, he raised his gray head. "Would the defendant rise?"

"Mr. Michaels, you are charged with murder in the first degree. How do you plead?"

Sean straightened his shoulders. "Not guilty, your honor," he answered in a strong, clear voice.

The judge looked to Paul Garner, the assistant D.A. "Bail, Mr. Garner?"

Paul Garner, a giant of a man, squared his shoulders and looked contemptuously at Sean. "The people ask for the maximum of two million dollars, your honor."

"But your honor," Khendra interjected, stunned by the monstrous ransom. "This request is excessive. My client is an upstanding member of this community. He is a leading member of the bar and a partner at one of the most prestigious law firms in this state. He is not a flight risk, your honor."

"Mr. Garner?" Judge Abramson looked at the assistant D.A. dispassionately.

"Your honor," Garner boomed, "this crime, to say the least, is a heinous crime. This man is violent and he still has ties outside of this state."

"Don't try your case here, Mr. Garner. You'll have plenty of time for that. I agree with defense counsel," he continued. "Bail is set at one hundred thousand dollars.

Sean breathed a sigh of relief.

Abramson flipped open the court calendar, then looked up, pushing his wire-rimmed glasses up on his bulbous nose. "Trial date is set for six weeks from today—nine a.m." He banged the gavel. "Next case."

Chapter Twenty-four

It had grown dark. AR of the tenants had left for the evening. It was quiet. The perfect atmosphere for the painstaking work that needed to be done. The jury had been selected and the trial was only days away. Yet, she was no closer to discovering the truth than she was when she began.

Khendra turned on the desk lamp and continued to sort through the stack of material in front of her. She had rented desk space from an old school friend who leased an office on a monthly basis. The arrangement would work out perfectly, she assured herself as she pored over the detailed accounts of the arresting officers and the officers at the scene. She leaned back from the desk and massaged her temples. Once this case was over, she would leave Atlanta for good.

Over. It sounded so final. Would it ever really be over between her and Sean? Would her disillusionment with love ever be over? It didn't really matter anymore, did it? She had made her decision. Love wasn't for her. She had her career to think about, and a case that was more important to her than any she had ever handled.

The awareness shook her. Was it because it was Sean? She didn't want to hear the answer that danced in her head. She wouldn't listen. She didn't want to give in to the shivery sensations that rippled through her when she remembered his touch, his lips, his scent lingering on her long after their explosive hours of lovemaking. She wouldn't give in to the heated fluid that sought release. She couldn't risk it. Not now. Not again.

Instead, she compelled herself to go over the list of tenants who were questioned and the evidence that the D.A.'s office had compiled against Sean.

She frowned. It didn't look good. Everything pointed to his guilt. Essentially, there was circumstantial motive, opportunity, and most damaging, there were witnesses who not only heard the violent quarrel, but who saw him enter and leave the building. Along with his own admission of being at the scene. But there had to be something she was overlooking. There had to be.

The one question that nipped at her mind was— why had the firm refused to defend one of their own? The only conclusion she could come up with was Alex.

Donna Hill

He was the impetus behind everything at MC&P. Just the thought of him resurfaced the burning anger and resentment that hovered on the edges of her stability.

She shook her shoulders as if to rid herself of an unseen weight. Concentrating on Alex would not serve any purpose other than to get her agitated again and distract her from the task at hand.

She drew her attention back to her notes and Sean's statements, but something still didn't quite fit. And her continual and pulsing thoughts of Sean did little to help her concentration.

≈≈

He thought spending sleepless nights in jail was the ultimate test of his endurance. But this was worse. She was so close. Barely a heartbeat away, yet she wouldn't allow him within spitting distance unless it had something to do with the case.

There was so much that lay unsaid between them. Things that it was time she knew—why he had really come to Atlanta, and what he was on the brink of discovering before—

Before. If only he could go back and put the pieces together. Now he was no better than a pariah. Even the powers that be who sent him to Atlanta acted like he didn't exist. And all because Carol was the daughter of a judge. Bradford was probably behind his ostracism—his own last attempt at restitution for his daughter's misdeeds, even at his ex-son-in-law's expense. He almost laughed.

Then, heaving a frustrated sigh, he rose from the rumpled bed. Leaning against the window frame, he looked out into the starlit sky, and immediately images of Khendra lying in his arms loomed before him. His arousal at just thinking of her was hard and swift, leaving him hungry with desire, startling him with its urgency. Never before had a woman been able to capture not only his body, but his spirit, his every waking emotion.

His heart pumped. He had to see her, to touch her, if only for a moment, just long enough to wipe out the nightmare from which he seemed unable to awaken.

⌘

The bathroom was still steamy from the shower she had taken, and was filled with the heady aroma of the jasmine-scented shower gel she had rubbed into her skin.

Wrapping her freshly-washed hair in a towel, she stepped out of the shower and padded through the small apartment. She had wanted to stay with Charisse, but Charisse's late hours and assortment of men were

too distracting. Much to Charisse's displeasure, she had fortunately found a reasonable sublet that would carry her through the period of the trial.

Temporary. The transient thought rippled through her brain. It seemed that everything in her life was temporary. No matter how hard she tried. Her success, her career, her love life, everything. Temporary.

Maybe that's the way things should be, she thought, trying to make sense out of the senseless. But didn't she deserve more than that? She had tried so hard, she thought, the ache of loneliness taking hold, as she stroked her body with her favorite cream. She glided her hands over her long legs, up to her thighs and across her firm belly.

Closing her eyes, she envisioned Sean's hands as they had caressed her, heated her, loved her, and the tears began to fall. One by one, they slid down her high cheekbones, dripping across her full breasts in a silent stream. All of the hurt, humiliation and heartache fought for release.

Soundless sobs shook her body as her hands instinctively sought to soothe the ache within her. Tender words of passion sprouted in her ears, a voice so lovingly low and thrilling it sent shivers of dreamy desire surging within her.

Sean. His name involuntarily slipped through her lips, willing his presence, electrifying her with its sound. Then her eyes fluttered open as an insistent buzzing pierced her erotic thought. Rising, as if from a dream, she pulled on a robe and went to the door.

Sean! It must be an apparition, she thought through the haze of her fantasy.

"Could I please come in, Khen? I...I had to see you."

She knew it was wrong, knew that this would only lead to her own undoing, but she seemed to lose all her own will when she looked into his eyes, and relented to the throbbing sound of his voice.

She stepped away from the door and let him in. He moved past her and the manly scent of him rushed through her veins, quaking her heart.

He turned around to face her, and all of his good intentions flew out the window. She looked so vulnerable, so soft, so hurt and uncertain. And the painful reality was that it was his fault. He had allowed his superego to overshadow his reason and he had lost the one person who meant more than anything else in the world to him. He took a cautious step toward her.

She flinched, pulling her robe tightly around her as if to ward off some unseen danger. But she didn't move away. Her heart raced. *Please don't. I don't have the strength to resist you. I need you so much...please stay away—*

He stepped closer, compelled by a force more

powerful than any he had known. And in the next breath, he gathered her into his arms, pulling her to him, his hungry lips brushing across hers in a feather soft kiss that denied the unbelievable urgency that whipped through his body.

Then with infinite care, he applied more pressure, stroking her cheek with a gentle caress. He felt her tremble and he pulled her closer, now demanding that her lips relinquish all resistance and melt the icy wall that had formed between them.

Her mouth slowly opened, hesitantly accepting his probing tongue. So sweet, she thought, the last vestiges of reason blowing away.

His hand reached up and loosened the towel that held her hair, and it dropped to the floor, as her still-damp hair cascaded through his fingers. A ragged groan eased from her opened mouth, as his hands slid down her back, tingling her spine, caressing her round buttocks. He pulled her closer, his hard masculine body thrust against hers, igniting the passion that throbbed within her.

She felt her knees weaken, her heart slam against her breast, as his agile fingers expertly released the belt that held her robe. His fiery hands eased beneath the fabric, stroking the inflamed skin that seemed to scorch his fingers.

A shudder ran up his back and he choked out her

name, his hands moving along the curves of her perfect breasts. She moaned when he massaged them with the pads of his thumbs. Her own fingers instinctively ran up his back, feeling the taut muscles that rippled up and down his spine.

His tongue probed deeply into her mouth, dancing, taunting, arousing, moving in a penetrating, ritualistic rhythm. Her own mouth competed with his, craving the blinding sensations that engulfed her.

This was wrong, she thought dizzily, a moment of rationale struggling for control. It wasn't supposed to be this way. Her thoughts swam in uneven currents. Too much had happened, too many lies.

His hand deftly roamed her body, sliding to the core of her womanhood.

She gasped. *I can't let this happen. I want him.*

"I love you, Khen," he whispered roughly against her mouth. "I've never stopped loving you."

I love you, too. Heaven help me, I love you too.

He lifted her from the floor, his eyes burning into her with a raw desire she had never before witnessed, frightening her with its intensity. His mouth closed over hers, stifling any words of uncertainty as he carried her into the bedroom.

Standing above her, he watched her still form, every muscle cord in his body straining. He wanted her so desperately, he couldn't think clearly. He knew that if he touched her, at this very moment, it would be over. And he wanted to take his time. He wanted to take forever.

She watched him remove his clothes, dropping them on the floor item by item, his strong chocolate-coated body shouting his virility.

She did not utter a word, but her eyes never left his face, as though searching for some explanation for the ethereal passion that flamed between them.

He lowered himself onto the bed, bracing himself above her on muscled arms. His eyes searched her face, saying all the words that raged within his heart. He lowered his head, his lips touching hers in shivery delight.

She stretched up her arms and pulled his head closer, crushing his mouth against her own. She flicked her tongue across his lips, searing them, gaining easy access to the depths within.

He moaned, as the flames rose within him. Reason fled, as he spread her satiny thighs with a well-placed knee, stroking her curves with unconcealed tenacity. His hot, wet lips wandered across her face, her throat, and down to her jutting breasts. She thrust her breasts against him, forcing them deeper into his heat-filled mouth.

The sensation was explosive as a myriad of brilliant lights danced and erupted before her eyes. Her fingers ran up and down his back, her ankles locking around his narrow hips, urging him downward.

She let her body succumb to the electrifying sensations that ripped throughout her being, forgetting the promises she had made, only wanting him, needing him, loving him at this moment with all of her being.

He wanted to devour her, hold her captive in this wonderland of bliss, make her forget the past, forgive him for his indiscretions and love him as he knew he loved her. He drank of her as a child draws on its mother for nourishment, relishing in the exquisite, bittersweet taste of her, relieving himself of all reason other than satisfying her as never before. This is how it should be, he thought, through the cloud of tempestuous awakening. And it always would.

Slowly he raised his head, looking upward to her face, seeing her enchanting face completely consumed in the throes of passion, which only intensified his own. His mouth spontaneously covered hers, capturing the outcry of his name as he locked them together as one, sweeping them away, demanding her accompaniment, extinguishing all barriers.

She clung to him as one sweet sensation after another rocketed through her supple body. She felt as if she were on a precipice, ready to fall off, the thrill of floating through the air, the danger of falling making her heart race in an uncontrollable rhythm. But she knew he would be there to catch her.

She moved beneath him, stroking him, rocking him within her. She cast aside doubts and misgivings, letting her body and soul guide her upward to the height she knew she would soon reach—and she knew, at that moment, that she wanted him with her.

Their ragged, whispered voices called each other's name in syncopated unison, the beat of its sound like an animal cry—savage, thrilling.

He pushed downward, slowly, relentlessly into her realm, seeking and finding the hot, liquid haven that enveloped him in a silken fire. Her fingers trailed up and down his back, softly, tenderly in places, urgently demanding in others, sending shivers of fierce yearning tramping through his throbbing, swollen loins. Her whispered, erotic words of encouragement spurred him further, clouding his sensibilities, blinding him to all but fulfillment for them.

Pure and crystal clear tears of intoxicating joy sprang from the corners of her eyes as his every motion swept her to greater heights. She couldn't breathe, her heart raced as his thrusts quickened, hurtling them forward to a place they had never been before. A secret, divine place where only true lovers met, a higher ground only known to those whose spirits have joined and united.

He so wanted to be there forever, to linger with

her on this pinnacle of tumultuous rapture, but he couldn't. No longer could his body withstand the torturous heat that was methodically catapulting him through space and time. A shudder of pure surrender raced through him as he relinquished his hold on earth and drew her undulating hips savagely against his. His mouth crashed down on hers, as explosion after explosion shot through him, her own contracting reply draining him, freeing him, heightening his release.

She cried out his name over and again, as shock waves of unbound deliverance ripped through her. The burning fluids of life filled her, satiated her, radiated within her, made her complete.

The world ceased to move, the air no longer blew. The only sound was two pounding heartbeats—beating as one.

Khendra rolled over and checked the bedside clock. It was nearly two a.m. Turning on her side, she watched Sean's sleeping form, his breathing slow and regular as though he didn't have a care in the world. The pastel blue sheet was twisted around his waist, exposing his broad chest and giving a brief hint of what lay beneath, bringing back the memories of the previous hours.

She turned onto her back and pressed her head into the fluffy pillow, staring up at the white ceiling. What in heaven's name have I done? She hugged herself as a chill of dread scurried up her body. Not only had she compromised her morals, she had compromised her ethics as well. She had slept with a client. If that fact was ever discovered—

She didn't want to think about the consequences. All she knew was that as momentarily beautiful as it was between them, it was wrong. Disastrously wrong. There was no way she could handle a relationship with Sean and be his attorney as well. Deep within her heart she had not forgiven him for being an accomplice to Alex's treachery. Whatever his reasons might be, there was no explanation. She had let her body distort her judgment.

He had betrayed her. Now his life lay in her hands. The troubling parallel frightened her. Would she reasonably be able to defend him, knowing her innermost feelings, or would she contribute to his downfall? The demons of doubt battled within her. She turned to look upon him once again, and her heart skipped a beat, the painful reality setting in. This was not the way to find out.

She reached over and shook his shoulder. He stirred, his eyes drifting open.

"What's wrong?" he mumbled, reaching out to

stroke her face.

She pulled away. "I want you to leave—now."

"What? What's wrong. I thought—"

"You thought wrong, Sean. This was a mistake. We're a mistake. And I'm going to correct it. I want you to leave."

Pain and confusion spread across his dark, handsome face, and his stricken look shot straight to her heart. But she could not back down, even though those incredible black pearl eyes clung to her face.

She got up from the bed and tossed his clothes at him, snatching up her robe in the process.

"Khendra, wait, we need to talk. I know everything happened so fast, but there's so much I want to tell—"

"I don't want to find you here when I get back," she whispered, her heart aching. "I'll see you in court on Tuesday," she added with finality.

She strode out of the room and locked herself in the bathroom, afraid that if she stood there a moment longer he would see right through her facade.

Silent, mournful sobs wracked her body as she heard the front door close behind him.

Chapter Twenty-five

The courtroom was packed. Reporters, television cameras and spectators filled the overheated room to capacity. The noise level was deafening, the flurry of activity chaotic.

The media was having a field day with this case. Every day since its occurrence, Sean's name had been blasted across the headlines. It was a miracle they were able to select a jury. Khendra felt sure she would have to get a change in venue, when finally, the last juror was selected.

She sat silently at the table, Sean's thigh pressing lightly against hers, making her nerves quake. They hadn't been in contact with each other since their night together—until today—and it was just as well. She would not have been able to concentrate. Her conscience and her emotions were in such turmoil, she had hardly slept in days. But somehow she had managed to put a case together.

She felt pretty confident that they had a reasonable chance for an acquittal, given the fact that no fingerprints could be lifted from the scarf, which could substantiate reasonable doubt. Her case hinged on convincing the jury that someone else was there that night, which would raise a reasonable doubt. At the very worst, she would work for a reduction of the charge. If he let her.

She dared to look at him. His hands were folded in front of him, still and unmoving. He looked straight ahead. But tight lines of tension rimmed his eyes, the only visible sign that this whole procedure was anything more than a stroll through the park. Yet, she knew better. They had discussed his chances earlier that morning and the risk he took by not accepting the deal offered to him by the D.A.

There was a surge of activity in the back of the courtroom and light bulbs flashed. Sean and Khendra turned toward the entrance door simultaneously, to see Alex Counts moving through the crowd shaking hands with the press as he walked.

Khendra's chest tightened.

Alex walked up behind them and leaned over the guard rail and clamped Sean on the shoulder. "Michaels, we're all behind you, one hundred percent. You know that."

Sean looked up into blue eyes and the false smile of encouragement. He felt like wringing Alex's neck. This blatant show of hypocrisy made his stomach turn. Ironically, Alex had escaped his downfall by the events of Sean's horrific nightmare. And Sean cringed when he thought how close he had been.

"Thanks, Alex," he said in a tight voice, turning away.

Alex nodded in Khendra's direction, by way of acknowledgment, and took a seat in the back of the courtroom, waving away the eager reporters with a "no comment." *And I'll be here every day,* he thought. *Right up until the end, showing my full support.* He quickly surveyed the room. The woman was nowhere to be seen. He smiled.

A hush fell over the courtroom as everyone was asked to rise, announcing the arrival of Judge Abramson.

The proceedings began.

Khendra listened to the prosecutor make his opening remarks, jotting down hasty notes and gauging the reaction of the jury. She didn't like what she saw.

Chapter Twenty-six

Khendra took a deep breath as the prosecutor wrapped up his opening statement.

"...Therefore, ladies and gentlemen of the jury, the state will prove beyond a reasonable doubt that this man," he turned and pointed an accusing finger at Sean, "is guilty of the murder of Carol Gordon-Michaels. Thank you."

His booming voice reverberated across the high ceilings, clamping the crowded room into absolute silence. He took his seat, his unspoken victory slung from his shoulders like a mantle.

Khendra slowly rose and walked to the jury box. She knew she had to pace her words and her movements with precision. It was imperative that she capture the jury from the start. She smoothed the lapel of her mauve-colored wool suit and began. Her nut-brown eyes swept across each of the jurors as she spoke in clear, measured tones.

"You've heard the eloquent words of Mr. Garner weave a tale of violence. But the one factor he forgot to mention was motive." Her eyes scanned the jury. "Motive, ladies and gentlemen. What possible reason could my client have for murdering his ex-wife? Was it a crime of passion? I think not. Was it robbery? No. The police officers found no evidence of robbery. We will prove that someone else was present that night. Someone known to the victim, and that someone was not Sean Michaels—"

By the end of her opening remarks, Khendra felt confident that the jury had been awakened to the possibility that someone else had been present that night. Now all she had to do was prove it.

❧

The first day of testimony was long and arduous. Statements by the officers on the scene and the arresting officers were not as damaging as she thought they would be. However, it did not look good that Sean had a bag packed at the time of his arrest. Paul Garner also introduced the witness who had found the body.

Tomorrow would be crucial. The prosecution was going to introduce the witness who saw Sean enter and leave the building.

As the court was, mercifully, called to recess until the following morning, Sean held Khendra's arm as they prepared to leave the courtroom.

"You were fantastic today." His voice stroked her.

She continued to pack her notes into her briefcase, not daring to look into his eyes. "Thank you. But I didn't think you hired me to do a lousy job. What you need to concern yourself with is tomorrow. The testimony of the tenant is what we should be worrying about."

She pulled away from him. "I've got some more work to do this evening. I suggest you go home and try to get some rest."

She turned away from him and walked out of the courtroom, her heart thudding in her chest.

≈≈≈

Day 2

"I heard a lot of commotion, things crashing to the floor and a lot of yelling and shouting," stated the elderly Mr. Harris.

"And what did you do when you heard all of this commotion?" asked Paul Garner.

"At first I didn't do anything. I thought it was a

lover's spat. Then I heard a loud crash, and then nothing. I waited a few minutes and then I looked through my peephole."

"Where exactly is your apartment in relation to the victim's, Mr. Harris?"

"Directly across the hall."

Paul Garner brought a diagram up to the witness stand and asked that the witness point out the locations.

"Your honor, I ask that this diagram be admitted into evidence as Exhibit A."

"Duly noted, Mr. Garner," intoned Judge Abramson.

Garner turned back to the witness. "And when you looked out, Mr. Harris, what did you see?"

"I saw a man running out of the apartment and down the stairs."

"Is that man in the courtroom now?"

"Yes, he is."

"Would you point him out to the jury, Mr. Harris?"

He pointed directly to Sean. "That's him."

A wave of voices rushed through the courtroom.

"Silence!" roared Judge Abramson, banging with his gavel. The courtroom quieted in degrees.

"Let the record show," said Garner, "that the witness has positively identified the defendant, Sean Michaels. I have no further questions." He smiled smugly and returned to his seat.

"Cross examine, Counselor?" asked Abramson.

Khendra approached the witness, smiling softly.

"Mr. Harris, you noted your age when you were sworn in. Would you repeat it for the jury please."

"Objection, your honor!" shouted Garner. "This question was asked and answered. What is the purpose of counsel's question?"

"Your honor, I do have a purpose to this line of questioning. If you'll allow me some leeway..."

"Overruled. Continue Ms. Phillips, but don't stray too far. The witness is instructed to answer the question."

"I'm seventy-five years old, and proud of it."

A chuckle went up in the courtroom. Khendra gave him a patronizing smile. "And well you should be, Mr. Harris. But when was the last time you had a physical examination?"

"I saw my doctor two weeks ago."

She briefly glanced down at the note pad she held in her hand and then looked up at him, giving him an enchanting smile. "And isn't it true, Mr. Harris, that your doctor discovered that you have glaucoma and it has severely affected your vision."

"Yes, but—"

"Just answer the question, Mr. Harris."

"Yes," he sighed reluctantly.

"And isn't it also true that the glasses you have been wearing were not sufficient to compensate for your loss of vision?"

He hung his head. "Yes."

"Isn't it possible then, that the man you saw leaving the victim's apartment on the night in question was not my client?"

"I suppose so," he answered in a near whisper.

"Could you repeat your answer loud enough for the jury to hear, Mr. Harris?"

"Yes, I suppose I could have been mistaken," he said grudgingly.

"Thank you. No more questions for this witness."

"You may step down, Mr. Harris." instructed Judge Abramson.

An audible sign swept through the courtroom, and Paul Garner was livid. He nearly jumped down his assistant's throat for not having that information. Their key witness had literally been disqualified as unreliable.

Khendra returned to her seat, and Sean reached out and patted her hand, holding her hostage with his look. She tore her eyes away.

One down, she thought, but we have a long way to go.

Alex returned to his office from the afternoon recess. He had plans to put into action, and soon. He reached for the phone and dialed, tapping his nails against the desk as the phone rang on the other end. Just as he was about to hang up, a burly voice answered.

"Yeah?"

"Mike, this is Alex. Listen, I have a job for you. Meet me in my office in an hour. You may have to take a little trip."

"No problem," Mike answered, patting the back of the woman who lay beside him. "I'll be there. You want to tell me what it's about?"

"The usual. I need someone out of the way for a while. Nothing permanent—but just for a while."

"Sure thing. See you in an hour."

As Alex leaned back in his seat and smiled, his intercom buzzed.

"Yes?"

"Mr. Counts, I just wanted to remind you about your flight for tomorrow morning. Your tickets have just arrived."

Damn! He'd all but forgotten about his business trip to New Orleans. There was no way he could get out of it now. But he had to stay on top of this case. After all, the company's reputation was at stake. He chuckled. "Stacy, I want you to do me a favor."

She hoped it wasn't another one of his shopping

requests. These past few months had been horrendous.

"I want you to put off whatever you have planned for the next week, and attend the trial for Michaels. I want him to feel assured that we're behind him in this."

"Of course, Mr. Counts," Stacy replied, somewhat perplexed by his request. He'd never asked her to attend a trial before. Why now?

"Oh, and Stacy, I want you to take notes."

"Of course, Mr. Counts," she responded by rote. He clicked off.

Day 5

Paul Garner stood in front of his table and called Dr. Douglas Morrison to the stand.

"Dr. Morrison, would you state your occupation for the court?"

"I'm a doctor of pathology."

"And you were the doctor who examined the victim, is that correct?"

"Yes, that's correct."

"And would you tell the jury your findings?"

"There was a high concentration of cocaine in her blood, and she had been hit in the head by a heavy object causing a large gash just above the temple." He pointed to the location on his head.

"Was that blow enough to kill her?"

"No, it was not."

"Dr. Morrison, what other findings did you make?"

"The victim had a silk scarf knotted around her neck."

Paul strode over to his table and produced a silk scarf, then returned to the witness box. "Is this the scarf?"

"Yes, it is."

"Your honor, I would like to introduce this as Exhibit B.9"

Stacy sat in the back of the courtroom and her breath caught in her chest. That looked like— No, it couldn't be. But the feeling of unease wouldn't leave her as she listened intently to the testimony. Something wasn't quite right and she racked her brain trying to figure out what it was. Something that the salesgirl had said. What was it?

"Dr. Morrison, what was the actual cause of death?"

"The victim died of strangulation."

"Was there any sign of struggle, Dr. Morrison?"

"We found skin particles under the victim's fingernails."

"And what were your findings with these skin particles?"

"The particles matched samples taken from the defendant."

"In your opinion, would those particles of skin be a result of scratches inflicted on the defendant by the victim?"

"That would be consistent with my findings, yes."

"One last question, Dr. Morrison. Was the victim conscious at the time of her strangulation?"

"No, she was not. The blow to the head knocked her unconscious."

"Thank you, Dr. Morrison. No more questions. Your witness, Counselor." Paul strode triumphantly back to his seat.

Khendra walked up to the witness box and looked the stately doctor straight in the eye. "Dr. Morrison, it is your testimony that the victim died from strangulation by that scarf." She pointed in the direction of the table that held the evidence. "Is that correct?"

"Yes, it is."

"Were you able to lift any fingerprints from this scarf?"

"No, we were not."

Khendra nodded her head and paced in front of the jury box.

"'So in other words you could not positively determine that my client used this scarf to strangle the victim?"

"No, I could not."

"What could have caused the blow to her head, Doctor'?"

"The lab report states that blood was found on a brass coat rack. Tests revealed the blood type matched that of the victim's. Also, the bruise on the victim's head had an imprint similar to that of a coat rack.

"And does the report indicate the weight of the coat rack?"

"Yes, the coat rack weighed thirty-five pounds."

"And is it your opinion, Doctor, that in this alleged struggle, my client lifted this thirty-five pound brass rack and struck the victim in the head?

"His fingerprints were found on the coat rack."

"Just answer yes or no, Doctor."

"No. I cannot say conclusively that he struck her."

"Isn't it possible then that during this struggle, the coat rack could have fallen, hitting the victim in the head?"

"Yes. It is quite possible," he conceded.

"Isn't it true that some pressure had been applied to stop the bleeding from the victim's head?"

"It appeared so from my examination."

"Your honor, I'd like to introduce this blood-stained cloth as Exhibit C." She brought the soiled wash cloth up to the witness stand.

"Doctor, did the lab test this cloth for blood samples?"

"Yes."

"And what were the findings?"

"The blood matched that of the victim's."

"Now, Dr. Morrison, you previously stated that the victim was unconscious at the time she was strangled. Yet here is physical evidence that attempts were made to stop the bleeding from the blow to her head. She obviously couldn't do it herself. So are you saying that my client attempted to revive the victim and then strangled her? Is that the action of a cold-blooded killer?"

"Objection! Objection, your honor. Counsel is asking the witness to presume the mind of the defendant."

"Sustained. The jury is ordered to overlook this last line of questioning. Counselor, you know better. Stay within bounds."

"Yes, your honor. No further questions for this witness." She breathed a silent sigh of relief as she returned to her seat. Even though the question was stricken, the jury heard it. And the seed of doubt had been planted.

Paul Garner reluctantly rose from his seat, feeling that his case was already lost. "The people rest, your honor."

"Very well. Due to the lateness of the hour," said Abramson, "this court will adjourn until nine a.m. tomorrow morning. Ms. Phillips, be prepared to call your first witness."

"Yes, your honor."

He banged his gavel and exited the court, his heavy black robe flowing around his large frame.

Sean turned to Khendra. "You were wonderful today. That was a nice piece of work. I couldn't have done better myself." He smiled gently and she felt the stab in her heart.

"I'm only doing my job, Sean," she said, forcing the knot out of her throat.

He lowered his gaze and looked away, wanting to grab her and shake some emotion back into her. He had ruined everything. But his pride wouldn't let him go crawling to her now, trying to explain. And right now, he didn't give a damn about any of it. It had all been for nothing anyway. And the irony was that he was only trying to protect her. Well, if she only wanted a platonic relationship, business only, then that's what he would give her.

Sean and Khendra shouldered their way through the throng of reporters and cameras and were ushered

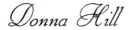

out of the courthouse by court officers, only to be assailed by more reporters on the steps.

"Ms. Phillips, how do you feel the case is progressing so far?" yelled one reporter.

"The case is moving along to our satisfaction," she stated simply.

"Why did you leave your law firm and then come back to defend an old associate?" the same reporter asked. Flash bulbs sparked in her eyes.

Her chest tightened. "I left the firm for personal and professional reasons," she said in a controlled voice. "And as for my return, I was asked by my client."

"Could you elaborate?"

"No, I cannot. Now if you'll excuse me." She brushed past the reporters, who then tried to converge on Sean. She automatically grabbed his arm, the contact sending jolts of electricity racing down her arm, as she pulled him with her down the courthouse steps.

"Let's go," she urged. "Where's your car?"

"I parked down in the municipal parking lot."

"So did I," she responded softly, feeling as though some unseen force had guided them both to the same spot.

They were the only ones in the lot when they arrived. Khendra walked in the direction of Sean's car and stood silently by the door. For a moment, neither of them spoke, the tension between them as real as the cold air that wafted from the pavement.

"I guess I'd better be going," she said finally, pulling her gaze away from him. She turned to leave.

"Khendra. Wait," he pleaded softly, the deep timbre of his voice tickling her spine.

She looked over her shoulder and her breath caught in her throat from the intimate look that held her.

"Yes?" She didn't recognize the tremulous whisper that was her voice.

He shrugged his left shoulder and looked at her through thick black lashes, going against all the promises he had made to himself. But if all he could have was platonic, then so be it. "I thought maybe we could grab something to eat...together."

"Sean, I—"

He held up his hand to stave off her rejection. "Listen, I promise no shop talk, no talk about you and me. I...I just want some beautiful company." He flashed her a shy, boyish grin that made her knees quiver.

What's the harm in dinner, she thought, dizzy with the idea of spending time alone with him again. Time that she knew was dangerously tempting, deeply provoking. Was she up to the challenge of his intoxicating charm?

"I have about an hour or so before I meet

Charisse. I guess it would be all right. This one time," she added by way of a warning. But to whom?

He smiled in relief.

"I'll follow you in my car," she said, nearly breathless from the look he flashed her way.

Chapter twenty-seven

"You went to dinner with him! Girl, have you lost your mind?" Charisse wailed in disbelief. Clad only in her underwear, she continued to wash the dishes that filled her sink, shaking her head as she rattled on. "You know every damn time you're alone with that man you lose it. And I mean that literally," she teased in a pseudo-male voice, flashing Khendra an all-knowing look over her shoulder.

Khendra burst out laughing, then let go completely, allowing the pure joy of laughter to wash over her, lightening her spirit. She laughed so hard, tears ran down her cheeks and she started to hiccup.

"Cee Cee, hic, you're just the medicine, hic, I needed." She wiped her face with a paper napkin that she picked up from the table, smudging her mascara in the process, and held it to her eyes until her giggles subsided. "But I must admit, you're absolutely right. I do

lose it every time we're alone together. And it just seems to get better and better. Hic." She doubled over in another fit of laughter.

"You got it bad, girl," Charisse chuckled, wiping her hands on the yellow kitchen towel as she sat down opposite Khendra. "But seriously, what's happening with you two?"

Khendra sighed deeply, sniffed back the tears of merriment, lowered her eyes, then looked up. "Nothing," she said in a bare whisper.

"Is that what you really want?"

"That's the way it has to be. It's just that simple."

"Is it? Why won't you just," she started holding up fingers as she went down the list, "one, admit that you're madly in love with this man, then tell him you love him; two, hear his side and forgive him; and three, walk off into the sunset so that you can stop torturing yourself and me? After you get him off this hook, of course." Charisse leaned on her elbow and waited for an answer.

"It's so easy for you, Charisse," she answered, getting up and spinning away from her seat, wrapping her arms around her slender waist. "I can't handle it. I've been hurt and betrayed by the people I love once too often. And anyway," she said in a low voice, "I don't think he'd tell me anything now. Not after the way I've treated him."

She turned to Charisse with hope in her eyes that Charisse would tell her something to allay her fears.

"Pride is a powerful thing, hon. But don't cut off your nose to spite your face." Charisse frowned. "Did Sean mention anything to you about doing all of this to protect you in some way?"

"No." Her heart pumped. "What did he say to you?"

"He just said he couldn't tell me everything, for the same reasons he couldn't tell you—for your own protection."

Khendra's brow creased. "What in the world could he be talking about?"

"The only way you're going to find out is to ask him."

Khendra twisted her lips into a fake smile. "Why are you so smart?"

"Somebody has to be in this outfit, or else we'd be up the you-know-what creek without a paddle." She planted her hands on her full hips and gave Khendra a wide-eyed look, which cracked her up again.

⤜⤝

"I'm going to crash out here on the sofa if you don't mind, Charisse," Khendra said, removing the back cushions. "I'm beat."

"Sure, there are some sheets and an extra pillow in the hall closet. Make yourself comfortable. The bathroom will be all yours in a minute." Charisse padded off to the bathroom and turned on the shower. "Try to get some rest tonight, Khen," she yelled over the rushing water. "You're going to need it."

"I'll try," she answered more to herself than Charisse.

Staring up at the ceiling after she had settled on the sofa, Khendra was filled with a mixture of hope and fear. Tomorrow was the last chance she had to get Sean off. Her only recourse was to call him to the stand, as much as she didn't want to. But she had no other choice.

She sighed. Things were going very well so far, almost too well. The thought left her with a very uncomfortable feeling.

Day 6

"Counselor, are you ready to proceed?" asked Judge Abramson.

"Yes, your honor. I'd like to call Sean Michaels to the stand."

They had prepared him for his testimony when they met that morning. His story never wavered and she was sure he would be able to convince the jury of his innocence.

Sean was sworn in and took the stand.

Khendra stepped up to the witness box, placing her hand on the railing.

"Mr. Michaels, I want you to tell the court what happened on the night of your ex-wife's death."

"I went to her apartment to see her, about ten o'clock, she said she needed money. When I arrived she was alone, dressed in this skimpy outfit. There was a line of cocaine on the table. I gave her the money and I was going to leave."

"Why didn't you?"

"She tried to come on to me."

Khendra inwardly flinched, but she held her emotions in check. "And then what happened?"

"I pushed her away from me and a planter filled with cocaine fell to the floor."

"Why didn't you leave then, Mr. Michaels?"

"I tried. I was at the door when she threw some scissors at me. They stuck in the door."

Khendra turned away from him and faced the jury as she spoke. "Tell the court what happened next."

He folded his hands in front of him and took a deep breath. "I turned around and she was coming at me, she had already scratched my face." He stroked the side of his face as an afterthought. "Then as she lunged toward me, she must have slipped because I moved out of her way and she crashed into the door. I was on the far side of the coat rack and I couldn't reach it in time. It hit her."

"What did you do then, Mr. Michaels?"

"At first I panicked. She was out cold and she wasn't moving. Then I ran and got a cold cloth and put it to her head. She was bleeding."

"Did she wake up?"

"No."

"Then why didn't you call an ambulance?"

He hung his head. "I didn't think. I just wanted to get out of there. I knew that when she woke up it would just be another scene."

"Mr. Michaels, to the best of your knowledge, was Carol Gordon-Michaels alive when you left her apartment?"

"Yes," he stated emphatically. "I know she was. I didn't kill her. She was breathing."

"Thank you, Mr. Michaels." She gave him a brief smile. She turned toward the judge. "I have no other questions for the witness."

Paul Garner fastened the button on his jacket and stepped up to the witness box, carrying a small package in his hand. Khendra felt disaster spreading through her. She gripped the edge of the table and prayed.

"Now, Mr. Michaels, you stated that you went to see the victim to give her money. Is that correct?"

"Yes."

"Why were you giving your ex-wife money? Was it an alimony payment?"

"Something like that."

"Just answer yes or no."

"No."

"Then would you explain to us why you were there to give her money?"

"She said she needed it."

Garner ran a hand across his cheek, and turned to face the jury. "I see. So you went to her house to give her this money. How much was it?"

"A thousand," he answered in a low voice.

"Could you repeat that?"

"A thousand dollars." His stomach clenched.

"That's an awful lot of money to give to an ex-wife. You must have had some relationship."

Chuckles wafted through the courtroom.

"Did she have reason to tell you why she needed this money?"

"No she did not."

His voice rose throughout the court. "Could it be that she was blackmailing you, Mr. Michaels?" He

turned and stared at Sean, waiting to pounce on him.

"Objection, your honor! Mr. Garner is asking my client to provide a motive for the victim's actions."

"Overruled. The defendant will answer the question."

"I don't know."

"Don't you? Well, I'd like you to take a look at these pictures and tell the court what they are."

Khendra saw everything crumbling at once. She had to find a way to salvage this case before it was too late.

"Objection! Objection!" She jumped up from her seat. "The prosecution is entering evidence that we were not privy to before trial. I demand a mistrial, your honor, based on prosecutorial misconduct." Her face registered stark outrage and icy fear.

"But your honor, this evidence was just brought to our attention minutes before the start of today's proceedings. We had no time to discuss this with counsel," Garner said in a patronizing tone. "I feel that these photos are very relevant to this case."

"Objection overruled, and your request for a mistrial is denied. Please have a seat, Counselor."

Garner puffed out his chest and laid out a series of photos showing Sean having lunch with, taking packages from and getting into a car with Leroy Gantz, one of the most notorious drug lords in the country.

Sean's heart pounded. For years he had dreaded this moment, and as much as he knew his innocence, these pictures were as damning as if what they reflected was accurate. He knew he was finished. Garner now had his motive.

"They are pictures of me making drug transactions," he finally replied in a low, tight voice.

An audible roar went up in the courtroom and reporters raced out to nearby phones.

Khendra lowered her head.

The next twenty minutes of questioning were more ruinous than if Sean had confessed. Her hands were tied. All of her objections were overruled and the courtroom was nearly in a state of pandemonium by the end of the day.

The assistant D.A. had questioned Sean about his marriage, his wife's drug addiction and the ensuing scandal of their divorce. Even though Khendra was able to re-direct, and have him explain what those pictures really meant, she was certain it was too late. She'd made a fatal error in not introducing this information herself, through Sean's own testimony.

With no more evidence and no more witnesses to call, she rested her case with a heavy heart. Tomorrow she would have to make her summation, and it would take every iota of know-how and passion in her plea for his acquittal to undo the harm that had been done.

✥

They stood silently in the parking lot facing each other, each knowing what the other was thinking. Khendra was the first to speak.

"I'll do everything I can tomorrow. I think you know that," she said softly.

"I know. We guessed wrong when we decided to put me on the stand. But things could still work our way." His dark eyes looked at her, filled with hope.

She pressed her lips together and merely nodded her head. "I'd better be going. I have a long night ahead of me. It's not too late to make a deal with the D.A., you know." It was a last ditch effort, but she was desperate.

"No deals! We agreed. I didn't do it, Khen, and I'm not going to cop a plea. If I can't get a full acquittal then—"

"All right." She placed her hands on his shoulders, wanting instead to hold him in her arms, but she knew that she couldn't. Then a frightening thought gripped her, and he seemed to read her thoughts as his eyes bored into hers.

This may very well be our last night together.

Her heart pounded in her chest and her blood

seemed to boil, as he lowered his head and brushed her lips with a feather-soft kiss.

"No matter what you think," he said huskily, "I've always loved you." He turned and strode away, his long legs carrying him swiftly across the pavement, and her heart went with him.

Chapter Twenty-eight

She waited the appropriate amount of time after the assistant district attorney's summation before she rose from her seat.

She stood before the jury, her eyes and her voice full of conviction. She knew that everything hinged on what she was able to make the jury feel. She smoothed the lapels of her dark green wool blazer.

"'Ladies and gentlemen, in order for you to find my client guilty, the evidence must show beyond a reasonable doubt that my client murdered Carol Gordon-Michaels. You were presented with the facts of this case. You were given evidence that has been negated. You have an eyewitness who cannot positively identify my client as the man he saw. You heard my client testify, under oath, that Carol Gordon-Michaels was alive and breathing when he left her. His only crime ladies and gentlemen, is being at the wrong place at the wrong time. You cannot, in good conscience, convict a man for that.

"The state has yet to prove that blackmail was the motive for this crime. My client is innocent until proven guilty. It was the state's responsibility to prove guilt and they failed. Can you, in good conscience, deny the possibility that someone else entered the victim's apartment and murdered her, after my client left? It has been documented that the victim was a drug abuser. There was plenty of evidence to attest to that. Isn't it possible then that her supplier is the culprit?

"When you go into deliberation, ladies and gentlemen, think. Think that the wrong verdict could put an innocent man in prison and the real murderer will still be among us. Thank you."

She gave the jury one last look and returned to her seat.

Judge Abramson instructed the jury on the laws and what their responsibilities were, then sent them into deliberation.

Exiting the courtroom, Khendra and Sean were bombarded by reporters and cameramen. The eager news hounds pushed microphones into Khendra's face, demanding her attention.

Donna Hill

"Please, Ms. Phillips, what do you think your chances are for an acquittal?"

"I believe we have presented a solid case and now we have to let the jury do its job."

"If your client is convicted, will you appeal?"

"Of course. But we're not looking for a conviction, the D.A. is. Please excuse us."

They pushed their way through the crowd and walked down the corridor to a vacant office. Khendra leaned against the door, breathing deeply.

"You did the best you could. That's all I can ask." He waited for her response.

She pushed herself from the door and walked to the window.

'This could take a couple of days," she said for lack of something better.

"I know that."

She felt him move up behind her. She held her breath. He pressed his temple against her head, deeply breathing in the fresh scent of her hair. A thousand thoughts crashed through his head at once. There was so much he needed to say, but he didn't dare. He couldn't take the rejection. Not again.

I*'m willing to listen this time*, she thought. *I've been such a stubborn fool. Please talk to me.*

"I guess I better be going," he said in a tight voice.

She felt her insides crumble into tiny crystal pieces. Her throat tightened. She nodded her head, afraid to turn and look at him, afraid to see him walk away. And then he was gone.

"When do you think you'll be coming back to New York?" Cliff asked as he tapped an impatient hand on his knee.

"I...I'm not sure. It's already been five days and the jury hasn't reached a verdict yet."

"How are you holding up?" he asked gently.

"As well as can be expected."

"Khendra, I—"

"Listen, Cliff, I really appreciate all your patience," she said gently. "It's more than I could ever repay. And I'll be back on the job as soon as this is over. I promise."

"I just want you to know that I'm here if you need me."

"I know. And thank you. I've got to go. I'll call you in a few days."

Cliff briefly shut his eyes as he hung up the phone, wishing that—oh hell, he didn't know what he wished.

≈≈≈

On the seventh day, word came that the jury had finally reached a verdict. Khendra got the call at her apartment and immediately notified Sean to meet her at the courthouse. She was never so overwrought with a case as she was with this one. Everything was all mixed up; her emotions, her legal responsibilities, her future.

She gunned the engine of her car and sped out into the teeming street, her heart feeling as if it were clutched in a vise. Snow flurries had begun to drift from the sky, as if to foreshadow an impending storm.

She met Sean in the parking lot, and together they walked to the courthouse. Silently, they entered the courtroom and took their seats.

"Would the defendant please rise," rumbled Judge Abramson.

Sean stood up with Khendra at his side. He straightened his maroon tie and buttoned the jacket of his navy blue pin-striped suit, inhaling deeply.

"Foreman, has the jury reached a verdict?"

"We have."

The bailiff took the folded piece of paper from the foreman and brought it to the judge. Abramson looked at the verdict impassively and returned it.

"What are your findings, foreman?"

"We, the jury, find the defendant..."

Everything was moving in slow motion. Sean heard the pulse pounding so loud in his ears he wasn't sure if he could make out what was being said. It seemed that at that moment his entire life loomed before him, braced to be altered, amplified, shared, lived. He looked briefly at Khendra and she instinctively turned to look at him. She touched his shoulder.

"...guilty of murder in the first degree."

Guilty. Guilty. Guilty. The word pounded through his head. Although he had thought he was prepared for the worst, the reality was almost more than he could withstand. He felt as if his whole being was plummeting into a nothingness, a dark void. He felt numb, alone, afraid.

The courtroom went wild. The judge pounded on the bench, demanding that the courtroom be cleared. Reporters swarmed through the doorway, pushing their way to the nearest phones. Several spectators were taken into custody, and after what seemed like an eternity, order was restored.

A suffocating sensation gripped Khendra by the throat. She still could not believe what she had heard. How could they not find reasonable doubt? She looked around the room in a daze, blaming herself. Every muscle in her body was stretched to the breaking point, and she felt that at any moment she would fall apart.

She had let him down. Just like she'd let Tony

down. What made her think she could win this case? Cliff was right all along. She was too close. She wasn't able to look at it objectively. And she had sent Sean to prison as sure as if she'd cast the final vote herself. Oh, God, what had she done?

She swallowed the knot that had lodged in her throat and dared to look at Sean as the judge announced when sentencing would take place.

He stood straight and tall, staring directly ahead, but his hands were balled into tight fists, the only outward sign of the torment that she knew hovered on the edge of overflowing. His once dark, beautiful eyes were completely vacant.

She tried to clear her head, to think quickly to try and fix it. But she couldn't. The shock of defeat was paralyzing.

"Sentencing will take place three weeks from today. Until such time, the defendant is remanded to the state correctional facility. Take him away."

Sean! Her mind screamed. *Please forgive me.* Her eyes followed him as he was escorted out. He looked over his shoulder and she could barely make out the words he mouthed as flashbulbs burst in her eyes.

"It's all right."

Chapter Twenty-nine

Stacy stared at her office phone. She had been struggling with her conscience for several days, ever since the verdict.

Maybe her suspicions were wrong, but she was usually on target when it came to seeing people for what they really were. And Alex Counts was the original s.o.b. All of her teen years spent hustling on the street had taught her to spot them a mile away.

He played a real good game, she thought, absently biting a pink nail, but she had seen through him from day one. What was worse, she had unwittingly helped him with some of his underhanded dealings. She had typed the false documents he had drawn up for clients, and for the large sums of money that were transferred in and out of his accounts. It was always she who went on the little shopping trips for his continuous string of mistresses—always under the guise that it was just another trinket for his "loving wife." The woman has to be a saint.

He thought he had picked the stereotypical "dumb blond" for a secretary when he hired her, and she played the role to the hilt, always acting none-the-wiser. But this was going too far and the implications frightened her. She couldn't sit back and pretend anymore.

She pulled her curly blond hair away from her face and reached for the phone, just as Alex marched through the door, giving her his usual grunt of a greeting.

"Damn!" She swore under her breath, while trying to look nonchalant. He was hours early. He wasn't expected back until late that evening. Now she would have to sit in his office and update him on what had occurred since his departure.

She would just have to make the call as soon as she was free. She knew she wouldn't rest easy until she got her suspicions off her chest.

Her intercom flashed.

"Yes, Mr. Counts?" she pulled sweetly.

"Bring in your notes from the trial and a cup of coffee, will you, Stacy?"

"I'll be right in, Mr. Counts." She made a face at the phone and rose from her seat.

Mistakenly, she thought that if she could keep her eyes closed, she could keep reality at bay. Yet, even in sleep, nightmarish visions of the guards leading Sean away played havoc with her nerves. The visions hung on the edge of her conscience, tormenting her, ridiculing her for her failure.

All of the jeering faces laughed at her, pointed fingers at her, and Sean stood in the midst of them all, sober, accusing her with those eyes of sable.

The torturous shadows loomed closer, and she felt herself struggling to fight them off. One dark hand reached for her and she sprang up in her bed, a cold sweat running down her back. She pressed the palms of her hands against her eyes, trying to force the relentless dreams back into the shadows.

The phone rang, and she nearly jumped out of her skin. She quickly gazed at the bedside clock. It was already noon.

The phone rang again. She even imagined it was more insistent this time, forcing her to respond.

"Yes?" she breathed, trying to draw on her last bit of strength.

"Ms. Phillips, this is Stacy Jeffries, Mr. Counts' secretary," she said in a husky whisper.

The hair on the back of Khendra's neck bristled. "I can't talk now," Stacy said, "but I need to meet you somewhere. I know things."

"What is this about, Stacy?" she asked, suspicion replacing animosity.

"It's about Sean Michaels."

Her heart skipped a beat.

"I have some information that I think can help you."

"Can't you tell me anything now?"

"No. I really can't. Please—just meet me. You name the place."

Khendra thought for a moment. "The Parrot Club. Do you know where it is?"

"Yes. I'll be there at one o'clock."

"I'll be there." Khendra absently hung up the phone, her brain rapidly trying to disseminate this latest development. What could Stacy possibly know that would help Sean? Unless—

≈≋≈

The jazz club-restaurant was dimly lit. Had it been later in the evening, it would have been full of customers and jazz aficionados. The Parrot Club was notorious for spotlighting the best jazz artists in the Atlanta area as well as the renowned greats.

Khendra had ordered a bottle of spring water and a chef's salad while she waited for Stacy's arrival. She hadn't realized how hungry she was until the scents of the home-style cooking drifted to her nostrils.

She took a bite of the salad, which was covered in blue cheese dressing, just as Stacy slid into the seat facing her.

"Ms. Phillips, we've never formally met, but I've seen you around the building," Stacy said, extending her hand, which Khendra shook. "I'm Stacy Jeffries. She quickly looked around as though expecting someone to walk up behind her at any moment. "I know that my phone call sounded real cloak and dagger, but I was just trying to be careful."

Khendra inhaled and leaned back in her seat, gauging Stacy with quiet caution.

"You said you know something about my client," she said in a low voice, raising a quizzical eyebrow. "Would you like to tell me about it?"

Stacy took another glance around the room, and took a quick sip of ice water. "I know things about Alex Counts."

Khendra's pulse began to escalate. "Yes?"

"That scarf that the woman was strangled with…"

Khendra nodded her head.

"…Well, about two months ago—"

Donna Hill

Khendra sped across the freeway, her brain traveling faster than the lightning-quick Volvo. She finally had a lead that made some sense. It was a slim lead, but at least it was a start. Now all she had to do was fit the rest of the pieces of the puzzle together. She pulled up in front of the Mirage Boutique that Stacy had told her about, pushed through the swinging doors and headed for the accessories counter.

Chapter Thirty

Khendra stood over Mr. Damato's secretary.

"I must see him. It's urgent. I have some information that is vital to my case."

"But Ms. Phillips, I just explained to you that he's busy," the young girl said in a polished voice. "If you could come back later—"

"What's all the commotion, Phyllis?" Ed Damato stepped out of his office, surprise registering on his face at seeing Khendra.

"Ms. Phillips? What are you doing here?"

"We need to talk. I was just given some very interesting information which could very well implicate someone else in the Michaels' case."

"Come inside," he said solemnly. "And Phyllis, hold all of my calls."

Ed Damato had been in the legal business for nearly twenty-five years. He prided himself on his

Donna Hill

record and on knowing when he had a good case. But this Michaels' case had disturbed him from the beginning. Yet, he had moved ahead, though reluctantly. Now, what was more disturbing, he may have been right from the outset.

Khendra explained what she had been told by Stacy, hope and ironclad determination rimming her voice. She knew she was hanging by a thread, but at this point she would try anything.

Ed leaned back in his chair, clasped his hands across his protruding belly and exhaled deeply. "It's not enough," he said finally. "The fact that Counts' secretary purchased a scarf that was identical to the murder weapon does not constitute enough evidence for me to reopen this case. Even the salesclerk's from Mirage statement that the scarf was a one-of-a-kind design, isn't going to cut it. You have to give me more."

Khendra rose from her seat, looking firm and resolute. "I will,'" she stated simply. She picked up her briefcase and walked out of the office.

As Khendra pulled her car out of the lot, she was busy planning her next step. She didn't want to say anything to Sean. At least, not yet. There was no point in getting his hopes up prematurely. But first, she had to take a short trip to New York. If her hunch played out, she'd have more to go on.

≈◎≈

The door chimes of the Gordon mansion tinkled in the background. Moments later, a middle-aged housekeeper appeared at the door.

"Yes?" the woman asked suspiciously, looking over Khendra's shoulder for any signs of reporters.

"My name is Khendra Phillips. I'm the attorney for Sean Michaels."

The woman tried to close the door in her face. Khendra pushed it back open.

"Please," she implored. "I just need a few minutes of Judge Gordon's time. I have some information about his daughter's murder."

"Mr. Gordon isn't talking to anyone. Now go away." She pushed the door again, this time with force.

Khendra shoved back. "Listen, if you'll just tell the judge I'm here, I'm sure he'll want to talk to me,'" she said, her voice rising in agitation.

"Cora. What is it?" came a deep voice from down the hall.

Khendra looked past the determined woman to see Bradford Gordon roll toward the open door in his wheelchair. She was surprised to see that he looked so robust and healthy. He had suffered a massive stroke years earlier and had retired from the bench. However, by looking at him, clad in a mint-green cable knit

sweater and dark gray slacks, one would doubt that anything could ever affect this powerful looking man.

"Judge Gordon, please, I need to speak with
you. It's about your daughter."

Cora stood rigidly at the door, ready to spring at
the direction of her boss.

"Let her in, Cora," he said in a flat voice. He
maneuvered his chair down the hallway and disappeared into one of the numerous rooms.

Khendra stepped past the reluctant Cora and
entered the enormous foyer. She was momentarily
overcome by the exquisite decor of the house. The
cathedral ceilings were inlaid with intricately-designed
tiles, which dropped dramatically to walls that were
covered in a rich damask fabric. The carpeted interior,
which was adorned with several brass urns containing
an overflow of brilliant plants, led to rooms on either
side of the hallway.

In the center of the foyer hung the most aston-
ishing chandelier she had ever seen. It appeared to
shimmer and dance with the light that poured in from
the floor-to-ceiling windows.

Cora took her coat and led her to a room where
Judge Gordon was seated near a French door that
opened onto the garden. The walls of the room were
lined with built-in cabinets filled with columns of
books.

"Come in, Ms. Phillips," he directed in his legendary deep basso voice.

Khendra took a seat on a low gray leather sofa. She smoothed her crimson colored, ultrasuede sheath and faced him.

"Judge Gordon," she began in a low voice. "I'll get right to the point. I need your help. I believe that I've come across information that may lead to the true murderer of your daughter."

She saw the pain that momentarily spread across his cocoa features, but it was quickly replaced by his notorious impassive look.

"I'm listening."

Khendra slowly and methodically explained what she had found out and her suspicions, presenting to him the statements made by both Stacy and the salesclerk at the boutique.

"What do you want from me, Ms. Phillips? I told the Atlanta police everything I know."

"Do you have any reason to believe your daughter was involved with someone?"

"The only thing she told me was that I was not to worry. She was being taken care of."

"Did she ever say by whom?"

"Carol was very secretive, Ms. Phillips."

"Were you aware that she was involved with drugs again?"

He visibly winced. "Not until I read the papers," he said in a nearly inaudible voice.

Khendra inhaled deeply before she dared to ask her next question. "What was her relationship with Alex Counts?"

For several moments she thought he didn't hear her question and she started to ask again, when he responded.

"He was her godfather." He was silent a moment before he continued as though looking back at his past. "Alex and I went to George Washington University together. We have been friends since childhood. When Carol was born, he took her under his wing as though she were his own. They had a very close relationship all during her growing up years. My wife, God rest her soul, said that it was too close. But I never listened. Alex is my friend," he added in a faraway voice. His eyes drifted off.

"Were you sending money to your daughter, Judge Gordon?"

He shook his head. "I told her to stay out of Atlanta. I knew that Sean was there and all he had been through after their divorce. I told her if she went, I wouldn't give her a cent. She said she didn't care, but she promised to stay away from him."

"Who would she have turned to?"

Silence.

And then finally in a voice filled with anguish and a frightened realization he said, "Alex."

"I know this is hard for you, but I believe an innocent man's life is at stake. Do you honestly believe Sean was capable of murdering your daughter?"

He simply shook his head, his eyes dark with loss.

"Thank you, Judge." She rose from her seat. "I believe I know who did, and I'm going to prove it." She strode from the room, her spirits lifted for the first time in months. But there was still so much to do, and time was running out.

Before she flew back to Atlanta, she stopped in to see Cliff to let him know how things stood and what she was doing.

"What makes you think you can prove such a thing?" Cliff asked incredulously.

"The pieces are coming together, Cliff. Can't you see that?"

"I think you're just hoping for some miracle. You really have nothing to go on. The D.A. will never reopen the case based on what you have. And where's your motive?"

"Too many things have been swept under the

rug, Cliff. And as for a motive ... I'll find one."

Cliff got up from his seat and paced the hardwood floor. "I hope you know what you're doing. If your suspicions are correct, you could be in danger. Did you think about that?" He turned to face her, the depth of his concern filling his eyes.

She briefly lowered her eyes, then looked up with stern resolve. "If it was your client, what would you do?"

She had taken the red eye flight out of New York to Atlanta. Her eyes burned from lack of sleep, and every bone in her body strained for release. But she couldn't afford to lose a minute. As she crossed the airport parking lot in the chilly morning air to get her car, her mind rapidly assessed all she had learned and her next plan of attack.

It was only six a.m. when she arrived at her office and began to re-evaluate her notes and the information from the police. There had to be something she had missed. She'd start from the beginning, with the tenants of Carol's apartment building. As she went over the names, something struck her. Gordon had said he'd given all the information he had to the police. Then why wasn't it anywhere in the reports?

Alex paced his office. He tried in vain to fight off the uneasy feeling that had been with him for days. His inside sources had told him Khendra was trying to have the case reopened and that new evidence was surfacing every day. He didn't like the sound of it, and he was going to have to do something about it.

He strode over to his phone and placed a call to Mike. He'd know what to do.

Khendra stood in the hallway of Carol's apartment building and looked over her list of tenants. Everyone's statement remained consistent with the information she had in front of her. She had spoken to everyone except a Mrs. Finch.

It was noted in the records that Mrs. Finch was not at home at the time of the murder. Khendra sighed and prepared to leave, then stopped midway the hall. What did she have to lose by questioning this woman? She turned back down the hallway and pressed the buzzer to apartment 2D, trying her luck.

Several moments passed and she was about to walk away, when a soft voice answered.

"Who is it?"

Donna Hill

Khendra's stomach tightened. "Mrs. Finch?" she asked through the closed door.

The door cracked open. "Yes?"

Khendra dug into her bag and produced her identification, holding it up to the small face that peered out. "My name is Khendra Phillips. I'm the attorney for Sean Michaels, and I'd like to ask you some questions."

The door opened a bit more and Mrs. Finch came into full view, clad in a plaid flannel bathrobe. She was in her late thirties, Khendra guessed, with dark brown hair and gray eyes that seemed to shimmer.

"What do you want with me?" she asked suspiciously.

"May I come in? Just for a minute. I only need to ask you a few questions."

Mrs. Finch hesitated a moment, then opened the door and let Khendra in. It was a comfortable apartment, decorated in soft beige and dark browns, with overstuffed chairs. Pictures of family members graced the walls. It was the kind of place you could call home, not like the other apartments she had visited that screamed money.

"Have a seat," Vera Finch offered.

"I don't want to take up too much of your time, Mrs. Finch—"

"Call me Vera," she said with a soft smile. "I

284

haven't been a Mrs. for quite some time," she added, feeling immediately at ease in Khendra's presence.

"Okay...Vera. I know you heard about the murder of Carol Michaels, and even though you weren't at home that night—"

"But I was."

"Excuse me?" Her heart pumped.

"I was home," she repeated. "Well actually, I was on my way to Florida that night. I just returned yesterday evening. But I heard all the commotion. I left for the airport about twenty minutes after the noise died down."

"Have you spoken to the police about this?" Khendra's pulse quickened.

"No."

"What do you remember about that night? Did you see anyone—this man?" She produced a photograph of Sean.

Vera looked at the picture long and hard, then shook her head. "That's not the man I saw," she said definitively. She returned the picture to Khendra, whose hands had started to shake.

Khendra swallowed the knot of pressure that had lodged in her throat. "Are you saying you saw someone else that night?"

"Oh yeah. He practically knocked me down the stairs as I was walking down to meet the cab that took me to the airport."

Khendra struggled to keep her excitement in check. "Do you remember what he looked like?"

"I'd never forget that face," she said, giving a slight shudder. "It was his eyes, they were a brilliant blue, almost electric, and he had thick steel-gray hair."

Khendra's mind raced. She quickly dug through her briefcase and pulled out the picture of Alex she had cut out of the company magazine. "Is this the man you saw?" She held her breath.

"That's him! I came out of my apartment and I had just reached the stairs when I heard someone behind me. I turned around and he was coming out of that woman's apartment. He rushed past me and I dropped one of my bags. He turned around to pick it up and he looked directly at me. It gave me a chill."

"Would you be willing to testify to that in court?"

"Is it going to get me in any trouble?"

"No. I promise you that. But an innocent man is going to go to prison without your help."

Vera studied Khendra's face and saw the intensity etched across her features. She believed her.

"I'll testify,'" she said finally.

"Thank you, Vera," she said, relief flooding her voice. "I'll be in touch in a few days. If you can think of anything else that might help, please call me." She scribbled her phone number on a piece of paper and handed it to Vera.

As she pulled her car away from the building, she was struck by the implications of what she had discovered. Alex was more devious than she could have ever imagined. Then Cliff's warning came back to her. "If your suspicions are correct, you could be in danger."

She couldn't risk thinking about that now. She had to see Ellen Counts.

❦

The wind stirred the statuesque oaks that framed the Counts' massive expanse of property. The early hours of twilight cast effervescent colors across the grassy lawn. Khendra drove down the winding driveway and pulled up in front of the house, briefly surveying the grounds. Alex lived well, she thought with disgust. And to the casual observer, one would never suspect the deviousness that went on behind those ornate doors.

She walked up the steps, raised the brass doorknocker and let it drop against the door. Almost instantly, a small but stately woman answered, presenting the almost untouchable air that comes with success and money.

"Mrs. Counts?"

"Yes." She looked at her quizzically for a moment. "Aren't you Ms. Phillips?"

"Yes, I am. I need to speak with you, Mrs. Counts. It's about your husband."

Ellen straightened her narrow shoulders and let Khendra pass, then guided her to what must have been a formal sitting room. The finely-furnished room was decorated in a Queen Anne motif, the dark wood and intricate designs of the furnishings taking one back to a more chivalrous time.

Khendra took a seat on the floral-patterned sofa, placing her briefcase next to her. Ellen walked over to a wet bar—which was totally incongruous with the room—and poured herself a drink.

"Would you care for something, Ms. Phillips?" she asked, more out of habit than cordiality.

"No...thanks. Nothing for me. As I said, I came to talk to you about Mr. Counts."

Ellen sat in a wing chair opposite Khendra and looked at her with vacant eyes. "What could you possibly have to say to me about Alex?" She took a sip of her drink.

"I have reason to believe he was involved in a murder, Mrs. Counts."

Her face was unreadable. "Really? Isn't that interesting." She took another sip of her drink.

Khendra was momentarily perplexed by her lack

of emotion, but plowed on. "Mrs. Counts, was there ever any reason to believe that your husband was having an affair?"

She chuckled mirthlessly. "I'm sure that he was, Ms. Phillips. There was always someone in Alex's life...other than me." Her pale lips thinned.

At least she was talking, Khendra thought. "Do you have any idea who she was?"

"They flit in and out of his life. There's never been anyone who lasted very long." She finished off her drink and returned to the bar for another.

"How do you know that?"

"Oh, the usual. Deductions from the checking account, usually to pay the latest one's rent, charge card receipts for women's items. Things like that."

"Have there been any recent deductions and receipts that you know of—over the past few months?"

Ellen gingerly walked over to a small desk and opened the drawer, then released a catch that opened a second draw underneath. She searched through several bundles of paper and pulled out the bank statements and a sheaf of receipts. Turning, she handed them to Khendra.

Khendra still couldn't quite believe the almost benign attitude of this woman, as she rapidly glanced through the papers. It was almost as if she had totally given up. And Khendra felt a pang of guilt at having to ask her these questions.

She carefully flipped through the papers. Then she saw it. For a three-month period there was the same deduction of nine hundred and fifty dollars—the exact amount of Carol's rent. She sifted through some more papers and found the receipt from Mirage. The scarf was the only purchase on the receipt.

Her pulse raced. She looked up at Ellen, who was looking blankly out the window.

"Mrs. Counts," she said gently. "I believe your husband was having an affair with Carol Michaels and that he murdered her." She saw Ellen stiffen, but she continued. "Where was he that night?"

"We went to a charity event," she stated simply.

"Do you remember what time?"

Ellen hesitated. "I know we were the last to arrive."

"Why was that, Mrs. Counts?"

"Alex...got home...late that night." She tossed the rest of her drink down her throat and turned to Khendra, the first flash of emotion registering on her face.

"Let me tell you something, Ms. Phillips. My husband has provided me with all this." She swept her hands expansively around the room and beyond. "He lives his life and I live mine. We like it that way. And if you think for a moment I'd risk losing it, then you're mad. As far as I'm concerned, this conversation never occurred. And I would appreciate it very much if you left now." She turned her back in dismissal.

"I may not need your help, Mrs. Counts, but I hope you sleep well at night knowing what your husband did to Carol and to an innocent man." Khendra snatched up her belongings and walked out of the house, somewhat relieved to be free of the oppressive atmosphere.

Hurrying to her car, she drove out of the driveway, unaware she had been seen.

✥

Alex marched into the house, slamming the door solidly behind him. "Ellen!" he roared, storming through the house, flinging open doors until he found her in the study.

She was sitting on the sofa, a ghostly pallor masking her face. She turned red-rimmed eyes upon him, her third drink shaking in her hand.

He crossed the room in two strides and knocked the glass from her hand, fury and a dark fear heightening his features.

"What was that woman doing here?" he demanded. "What did you tell her?"

"I didn't tell her anything," she answered weakly.

"You're a liar!" His large, open hand connected solidly with her face, knocking her to the floor. She tearfully told him what he wanted to know.

Enraged, he saw all of his life crumbling around him, just the way his father's had when he was betrayed by Alex's mother. He raised his hand again, and Ellen cowered. As he administered blow after blow, he avenged his father and the infidelities he had been subjected to by his mother. *"All women are alike. They needed, wanted someone to control them or else they would destroy you."* He heard the words of his father ring in his ears. And he wouldn't let a woman destroy his success.

❧

The following morning, Khendra sat alone in her rented office space, meticulously detailing and analyzing all the information she had gathered. Hovered over her desk, she didn't realize anyone had come in until a shadow loomed across her desk.

Startled, she looked up, only to find Ellen Counts standing in front of her. She wore all black, which made her small frame seem even smaller. Her look was almost ominous. A sheer black scarf covered her chestnut brown curls, and her eyes were hidden behind wide dark glasses. She looked as though she were on her way to a funeral.

"Ms. Phillips," she began weakly before Khendra could speak. "I'm willing to testify against my husband." She slipped the glasses off her nose to reveal large purple and black bruises around her eyes and a jaw that seemed grotesquely swollen.

Khendra sprang from her seat and rounded the desk, sure that if she didn't catch Ellen she would collapse. She gently lowered her into a nearby chair.

"Mrs. Counts, what happened?" Khendra reached out and instinctively touched Ellen's cheek.

"He beat me," she said, tears welling in her eyes. "And it's not the first time." She lowered her head. "It's been going on for years." She took a deep breath. "I can't live like this anymore. I'll do whatever you want."

❧

Hours later, Khendra packed up her notes and placed a call to the D.A.'s office, advising him she had all the evidence she'd need to have the case reopened. She told him she would be at his office within the hour.

Her spirit was lifted, her heart light with hope as she drove down the winding highway. After she saw the D.A., she would go see Sean and tell him the good news.

Sean. It seemed an eternity since she'd seen him. And she didn't realize how badly she missed him until now. Where had things gone wrong? Where had they gone wrong? So many things had gotten in the way of their love. Maybe it just wasn't meant to be.

She picked up speed, casting aside the disturbing thoughts, only wanting to see the look on Ed's face when she showed him what she had. She turned the car around the biting turn and the car seemed to accelerate. She stepped on the brakes. Nothing happened.

Sheer, dark fear assaulted her as she fought with the wheel, slamming down on the brakes to no avail. The car seemed to have a will of its own as the speedometer rose.

She screamed as the car veered around a curve, and the last thing she remembered before the car careened into the ravine was...Sean.

Chapter Thirty-one

She floated upward through the heavy clouds that surrounded her, a deep pain that she couldn't understand seeming to hold her down.

A low groan filtered through the air, and she couldn't tell where it came from. Slowly, painfully, her eyes fluttered open only to shut again against the glaring fluorescent lights. She tried to move, but every bone in her body felt as though it were on fire, and she panicked as darkness threatened to engulf her once again.

A low voice drifted to her ears, pulling her back to consciousness. "Ms. Phillips, can you hear me?"

She struggled to open her eyes and force her lips to form words, but she couldn't.

"Ms. Phillips." The voice pounded against the ache in her head. "I'm Doctor Roberts. You're going to be just fine," he assured in a soothing bedside tone.

"You're in the hospital. You were in a car accident."

Flashes of the car hurdling over the divide rushed to the surface. A strangled cry bubbled up from her throat.

"Don't try to talk," the doctor urged, placing a calming hand on her bandaged shoulder. "You sustained a concussion and some cracked ribs. And your shoulder was also dislocated."

"Water," she whispered in a cracked voice.

Dr. Roberts reached over to the bedside stand and poured a small cup of water. He gently raised her head, allowing her to drink.

Resting back on the pillows, she slowly absorbed the doctor's words, the reality that she had survived finally sinking in. Then through the fog of awakening, her reasons for being on that road came surging back. How long had she been here? What about Sean?

"Doctor," she rasped, "how...long..." Her voice trailed off.

"You've been here three days. You're going to have a whopper of a headache for a while. We're giving you something for pain intravenously."

"I've...got...to get...out...my case...Sean." Her eyes briefly drifted closed.

Dr. Roberts frowned. "Sean? I don't understand. Was there someone else with you?"

She barely shook her head, as a blinding pain

roared through her skull. "Please." She stretched a weak hand and grabbed the cuff of his white coat. "Call District Attorney...Damato. Tell him to come."

"I'll do that first thing in the morning, Ms. Phillips."

"No. Now." Her voice was a ragged plea. "Please...it's urgent."

He was instantly alarmed by her growing agitation. "All right, all right. Just calm down. Nurse! Bring me five cc's of Demerol."

Within moments the sedative had dripped through the I.V., lulling Khendra into a dreamless sleep.

The next morning her thoughts were more coherent and the pain in her head had lessened to a dull throb. She tried to sit up, but the effort was too much and she collapsed back against her pillow.

She blinked her eyes and slowly looked around the room to see Ed Damato dozing in a chair by the window. She called out to him, relieved that her voice sounded almost normal.

He briefly shook his head at the sound of his name, and slowly rose from his perch. "How are you feeling?" he asked gently, approaching her bed.

"Like I've been run over by a truck." She tried to laugh, but it stuck in her throat.

"You're a very lucky young lady. Some tourists saw your car go over the divide and into the ravine.

They flagged down the highway patrol."

"My notes...on the case...where are they?"

"Safely tucked away in my office. You have a helluva case against Counts. But I have some bad news."

She braced herself.

"Your witness, Mrs. Finch, she's disappeared. And the sentencing is in six days."

Khendra closed her eyes as her head began to pound. Without Mrs. Finch, the entire case would fall apart.

"We have to find her," she croaked.

"Well, until we do, this whole thing is at a standstill, even with the wife's testimony, which she could back out of at any minute."

She tried to think. There had to be something she could do. Then she remembered Phil, Sean's friend.

"I need you to call someone in New York. His name is Phil Banks. Tell him I need him. His number is in my book at the office." She leaned back, breathless.

"I'll have someone get right on it." He moved away from her bed, then turned back. "I've requested that a police guard be posted outside your door."

Her brow creased. "Why?"

"Your car was tampered with, and we don't want anything else to happen to you."

She shut her eyes against the quiet terror that crept through her bones. When she next awakened, a new day's sun had spread through the window and reality resurfaced.

I have to contact Sean. She reached for the bedside phone.

Charisse sat nervously facing the sheet of glass, watching the prisoners take their places in the booths. Her eyes searched the faces of the entering men as she looked for Sean.

Then she saw him. His still-confident swagger brought him in her direction. She was, once again, struck by his incredible good looks. Even the beginning stubble of a beard shadowing his chiseled face couldn't diminish his appeal. Rather, it enhanced his aura of virility, even in the dismal atmosphere.

Surprise registered on his face, and a feeling of foreboding floated through him when he saw Charisse. Why was she here? He sat down and picked up the phone. Charisse picked up hers.

"Where is Khendra?"

Charisse gauged her response, not wanting to upset him. "First, before I say anything, I just want you to know that she's going to be fine."

The muscle clenched in his jaw.

Charisse took a calming breath before she continued. "She was in a car accident."

"What! Oh, my God!" Alarm rang through his voice.

"But she's all right," Charisse assured. "She asked me to let you know that she has secured evidence to have the case reopened. The D.A. has it now."

His tightened shoulders slowly relaxed.

Charisse looked pensively at him, and he felt a but coming.

"The bad news is," she continued, "that her witness has disappeared. Khen had the D.A. contact your friend Phil. He's already in Florida trying to find the witness. Khen is positive she went back there to her mother's home."

"When will Khendra be released from the hospital?" he wanted to know, casting his own troubles aside, thinking only of her.

"The doctors say a few more days. She has a concussion and a couple of cracked ribs."

He briefly shut his eyes, pushing away the painful vision of her lying helplessly in a hospital bed. His stomach twisted. "Would you tell her something for me, Charisse?"

"Of course. What is it?"

"Just tell her that I know she did everything she

could and not to worry about me, I just want her to get well. I'm fine. Let the D.A. handle it from here."

"I'll tell her, but you know Khendra. She has a will of her own." She gave him a weak grin.

"Yeah, I know," he said somberly.

⋙⋘

Fighting the aches in her body and the flashes of pain that ripped through her head, it had taken Khendra nearly an hour to get dressed. But finally she was finished. She took her personal belongings from the bedside stand and dropped them into her handbag.

The doctor had said she needed to stay another week, but time was running out. Against all of the doctors' orders, she had signed herself out of the hospital.

Phil had called that morning to say he had located Mrs. Finch, but she refused to return to Atlanta. He said she was terrified. She had no other recourse but to go to Florida herself and beg her if she had to. She didn't care what it took, but Vera Finch was going to testify.

⋙⋘

The cab pulled up in front of a small whitewashed house, set back against a tiny grove of budding orange trees. Khendra checked the address against the one written on the slip of paper. Satisfied, she paid the driver.

The long ride from the Palm Beach airport had left her achy, and her head had, once again, begun to pound. Gingerly, she stepped out of the car into the blazing afternoon sun, and she had to quickly don her dark shades. Slowly, she made her way to the front door and rang the bell.

Within moments, a young girl, about eight years old, answered the door, looking at Khendra with startling gray eyes. The resemblance to Vera was astounding, she thought, seeing Vera as she must have looked as a child.

"Is Vera Finch here?" she asked gently, looking down at the girl.

"M-O-M!," the child yelled. "A lady is here to see you," she chanted.

Several moments later, Vera appeared at the door, shock and cold fear registering on her face.

"Kerry, go inside," she instructed her daughter. Then when Kerry was safely out of earshot, she turned to Khendra. "What are you doing here," she hissed. "I already told that man I wasn't coming back." Her cheeks flamed. "Now go away!"

"Vera, please," Khendra begged. "You've got to listen to me. A man's life is at stake."

"My life is at stake!"

Khendra's eyes immediately flashed concern. "Please Vera, let me come in so we can talk. What happened and why do you think you're in danger?"

Vera stepped aside, and Khendra walked into the small living room. Glad to be inside because her head was beginning to throb again, she sank into the first chair she saw. Vera sat down on the edge of the sofa, next to her.

"About a week ago, I received a letter stuffed under my door. I opened it and it was a note made up of letters clipped from a magazine or newspaper or something." Her hands started to shake.

Khendra reached over and patted her knee. "Go on, Vera. What did it say?"

"It said if I said anything to anyone, I'd regret it. And my..." the words caught in her throat," daughter would be harmed first." A slow trickle of tears ran down her cheeks.

"Vera, listen to me. I know you're afraid."

"You don't know anything!" she screamed, leaping up from the sofa. "What would you know about losing someone, the fear that they won't be there tomorrow? You, with your high-paying job and fancy clothes," she sneered. "What would you know? Tell me!"

Khendra swallowed back the knot of pain that

caught in her throat. The agony of Vera's words ripped through her, clouding her dark brown eyes—words more powerful than the pain that assaulted her body.

"I know," she whispered. "And I'm about to lose again, without your help." Her eyes and her voice implored Vera to understand.

Vera wiped away her tears, seeing in Khendra's face the mirror image of her own lost hopes and new-found fears. She hugged herself, willing her body not to crumble.

"What about my Kerry," she asked in a shaky voice.

The light of hope filled Khendra's eyes. "I'll arrange protection for both of you. I promise you that."

Agonized seconds passed.

"I'll go," Vera said finally.

Chapter Thirty-two

With Vera and Kerry safely tucked away and Vera's statement documented, the D.A. moved ahead with the warrant.

"...and Max," he said into the phone, "I also want a court order to have his bank accounts seized and all of his charge card receipts. Got it? Now move on it." He hung up the phone and looked up at Khendra.

"Now we just wait, and hope that he doesn't get wind of it."

Khendra stood with her hands folded in front of her, her face resolute. She simply nodded her head.

Alex leaned back in his chair, his feet up on the desk, a look of contentment covering his face. Everything had worked out smoothly, he thought, and by tonight he would be gone.

He picked up his plane tickets from the desk and inserted them into his inside breast pocket, patting it assuredly. He reached over and picked up a small bag, swung his legs to the floor and headed for the door.

Ellen Counts watched, with a mixture of fascination and regret as a half dozen police officers went through her house. She could call Alex and warn him. But then again, why should she? Maybe now she could begin to live.

The flight to Rio was scheduled to leave in twenty minutes. *Right on time.*

The boarding call was announced. Alex moved easily through the crowd up to the gate, handed the stewardess his boarding pass and made his way across the ramp.

There was a flurry of activity behind him, and he turned. Three men were pushing their way through the line, causing squeals and curses from the passengers.

Alex froze as they rapidly approached and encircled him.

"Alex Counts, we have a warrant for your arrest."

"There must be some mistake," he said, panic holding him immobile.

"I don't think so, Counts," Ed Damato said, seeming to appear from nowhere and moving steadily toward him.

"Cuff him, Murphy, and read the man his rights." He turned around, in disgust, and walked toward the exit.

※

Sean stood silently next to Khendra as she waited for the cab to take her to the airport.

"So what are you going to do now?" she asked, daring to look in his eyes.

He shrugged his shoulders and gave her a half-smile. "Try to start somewhere else, I suppose. I've had some offers."

She lowered her eyes. "Oh."

She doesn't want to hear it, he thought, misery enveloping him.

Please talk to me, she prayed, picking up her bag as the cab ground to a halt at the curb.

He walked her to the car, feeling as though his whole world was coming to a rapid close.

She stepped into the cab and looked up at him one last time. "Take care of yourself." She gave him a tremulous smile, her heart quaking in her chest.

"You do the same."

He grabbed the door, all the words he wanted to say fighting for release. But his pride wouldn't let him say them. "I...I just want to thank you for everything you did."

His beautiful eyes and unforgettable face etched themselves into her memory.

"You're the best." He leaned down, placed a feather-soft kiss on her brow, and whispered, "Maybe we'll see each other again."

She gently closed the door and the cab sped away, leaving her heart behind.

Chapter Thirty-three

One Month Later

Cliff and Khendra sat at a cozy little table at Tavern on the Green. The food was excellent, the music perfect and Khendra appeared more beautiful than ever.

The black, off-the-shoulder, sweetheart neckline dress hugged her every curve. Her shimmering auburn hair was swept up in a classic chignon, with tempting tendrils shadowing her face.

He longed to reach across the table and touch her. But she looked so fragile, almost too exquisite to be real. Yet, she was different since she'd returned—more reserved, withdrawn. And he knew it had to do with Sean.

They had spent every evening together since her return, but she was never really there. Her entire being

Donna Hill

was with Sean, and the quiet knowledge shook him.

He reached across the table and touched her hand, wanting to bring her back from that secret place to which she constantly escaped.

She looked at him with a distant smile.

"Khendra," he began slowly, "I know these last few months have been hard on you—"

"Cliff don't. I—"

"No. I want you to listen to me," he said in a husky voice. "You've been working like a demon for weeks. Almost as though your work could replace whatever it is you think you've lost."

She looked away, as the truth of his words edged up to her throat.

"I thought I could fill the gap, but—"

"Cliff, I—"

He put a gentle finger to her lips. "Ssh. Just listen. I know better now. I can't be what you want. At least not until you get rid of the ghosts."

Her lips trembled as she fought back her tears.

"I'd like to offer you a proposition. I have a little cottage in Nassau. It's quiet, secluded, the perfect place to relax and think."

He reached into his jacket pocket. "Here, I want you to take this." He handed her a key. "It's yours for as long as you want it. And I won't take no for an answer." He smiled at the look of gratitude that lit her eyes. "You could use some time off, anyway."

≈≈≈

The moon hung low in the sky, filling it with a brilliant white light. The crystal blue waves gently lapped against the white, sandy beach, caressing her slender ankles as she walked along the shore.

It had been nearly two weeks since she had sought refuge at the cozy hideaway. Still, the serene atmosphere hadn't soothed the tumultuous thoughts that continued to plague her.

Cliff had been so right about so many things. He was a good man, a solid man, one who could very well make her happy.

If...

If Sean had never entered her life.

But there were still so many unanswered questions, so many things left unsaid between her and Sean, and the hurt of his betrayal still lingered.

But she had been so stubborn. So consumed with her own hurt pride that she had not allowed him to reenter her heart. At this moment, as she looked up at the star-filled sky, she would give anything to have a second chance.

Sighing, she placed a brightly-colored beach towel on the sand and sat down, crossing her long legs beneath her. She stared out into the ocean, willing her-self back through time to a place that was filled with loving words and promises of a bright tomorrow. She covered her face with her hands—and she cried.

～～

With determined strides, he walked up to the moon-washed, wooden door. He raised his hand to knock, only to find that the door swung open at his touch.

He called out, but no one answered. Daring to enter, he crossed the threshold and walked through each of the rooms, finding each one of them empty.

His briefly-lifted spirits sank. Perhaps he'd made a mistake by coming at all.

With no real direction in mind, he turned to leave and walked aimlessly across the beach. Looking across the horizon, he stuck his large hands into the pockets of his white cotton slacks, wondering whether he should return to his hotel room.

His eyes trailed across the beach and languidly rested on a silhouette that made his insides tighten. The solitary figure looked so forlorn and lost, so much like he felt at that moment.

He moved closer and saw, captured in the glow of the moonlight, hair that seemed to reflect its rays in an iridescent dance. His breath caught.

Then, casting all doubts aside he slowly approached.

"Hi."

The voice shimmied down her spine and warmed her like heated brandy. She dared not look around, for certainly it must be her imagination. But it couldn't be, she realized as the familiar scent reached her nostrils.

She turned and looked up into eyes of black midnight, and her world stood still.

Chapter Thirty-four

He stood above her, as regal and sleek as a Nubian king. His skin of ebony glistened against the stark white shirt that was opened just enough to make her imagination run rampant.

Bubbles of joy danced in her stomach and lit her eyes, making the tears that still filled them shimmer in the moonlight.

"I came all this way for some beautiful company. It gets kind of lonely when you're new in town." He smiled hopefully at her, melting her heart, and she reached up to take his hand, drawing him down next to her.

She stroked his face, as though not believing he could be real, searching his eyes to be sure. Then all of her pent up feelings seemed to overflow at once. "Oh, Sean, I'm so sorry. Sorry for everything. I've been—"

"Don't," he said in a low voice. "It was my

fault. I should have told you everything from the beginning. But I was just afraid that if you knew too much, it might put you in danger."

She looked quizzically at him. "I don't understand," she said in a hushed voice.

He looked into her eyes. "Are you willing to listen to me this time?"

She bit her bottom lip and nodded her head.

He inhaled deeply, and then spun out the details that had led him to Atlanta and to her.

"It had come to the attention of the Bar Association that Alex was promoting unfair hiring practices as well as falsifying legal documents for large sums of money."

"Where did you fit in?"

"After my divorce and the near destruction of my legal career, I went into a small private practice in New York. Shortly after that, I was approached by a representative of the Bar to investigate MC&P, primarily Alex Counts. They figured that with my qualifications and with an opening coming up at the firm, I was the perfect candidate. So I applied for a position."

"And Alex hired you."

"Exactly, and he played right into my hands—he did everything he was suspected of doing, including pulling the rug right out from under you for not bending to his wishes."

"But didn't the other partners know what was going on?"

"If they did, they never let on. Alex can be a very intimidating and convincing man."

He took a deep breath and continued. "I finally had all the evidence I needed when—" He exhaled. "At least he got what he deserved. And he'll be disbarred."

She squeezed his hand, then looked up at him. "And all along I thought I was the one who had been wronged," she said mournfully.

Then the stark reality of his miraculous appearance dawned on her. "How did you know where to find me?"

"Cliff called me." His voice dropped to a low rumble. "And he told me if I lose you again, he won't give up as easily next time."

Her heart mellowed at the thought of Cliff's unselfish act. He was willing to give up his hopes for them just to see her happy.

"There will never be a next time," she said, her voice filled with promise. Her eyes held his.

He reached across and ran his fingers through her hair. "It's over now. Behind us."

She looked down at the sand. "Can you ever forgive me for being so foolish?"

He dipped his head to reach her mouth and let his lips answer her, surrendering his soul to the sweetness of them.

❧

    All the months of cruel anguish diminished bit by bit, like so many particles of sand blowing away with the tropical breeze, as he pledged his undying love.

    She clung to him, drawing on him for all the strength and solace her spirit craved. She gave herself up to his caress as his tender hands glided down her bikini-clad body, pulling her strongly against him, sending wave upon wave of longing surging through her.

    She tossed aside the ghosts that had stalked her happiness and, at last, put Tony's memory to rest, opening her heart completely and irrevocably to the man who made her life worth living again.

    She had recaptured love, and came to fully understand the true meaning of friendship, all under one blissful, moonlit night. And she vowed against his tender lips, never to let go again.

    Ever.

A NEW BEGINNING...

MCK